The name was ⬛⬛⬛⬛ in his heart.

Sophie reached out and closed her hand around Alex's arm. He opened his mouth but no words came out.

And she gasped.

"What, Sophie?" he murmured.

"I don't know what it is about you—" she stopped, licked her lips "—that makes me compelled to say some really bizarre things." Her eyes grew slightly unfocused as she reached up and rubbed her temple. "Humor me for a minute. Who is Jack Runningwater?"

The name was like a blast of cold water in his face. "My father," he mumbled. He had to get out of here. She was beautiful, and she wasn't his usual type. But she'd bewitched him. He was angry with her. He didn't trust her. He did not, could not, be even the slightest bit attracted to her.

For God's sake, she knew something....

TRACY MONTOYA

TELLING SECRETS

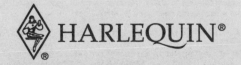

HARLEQUIN®

TORONTO • NEW YORK • LONDON
AMSTERDAM • PARIS • SYDNEY • HAMBURG
STOCKHOLM • ATHENS • TOKYO • MILAN • MADRID
PRAGUE • WARSAW • BUDAPEST • AUCKLAND

This one's for Kim and Sharron, for regularly talking
me down from the writer's ledge. It'd be lonely on
my freaked-out planet without you two.

And to Gail, Eileen, Lisa, Lena and Sandy for great
critiques and even better margaritas.

ISBN-13: 978-0-373-69299-6
ISBN-10:   0-373-69299-4

TELLING SECRETS

Copyright © 2007 by Tracy Fernandez Rysavy

ABOUT THE AUTHOR

Tracy Montoya is a magazine editor for a crunchy nonprofit in Washington, D.C., though at present she's telecommuting from her house in Seoul, Korea. She lives with a psychotic cat, a lovable yet daft lhasa apso and a husband who's turned their home into the Island of Lost/Broken/Strange–Looking Antiques. A member of the National Association of Hispanic Journalists and the Society of Environmental Journalists, Tracy has written about everything, including Booker Prize–winning poet Martín Espada, socially responsible mutual funds and soap opera summits. Her articles have appeared in a variety of publications, such as *Hope, Utne Reader, Satya, YES!, Natural Home* and *New York Naturally*. Prior to launching her journalism career, she taught in an underresourced school in Louisiana through the AmeriCorps Teach for America program.

Tracy holds a master's degree in English literature from Boston College and a B.A. in the same from St. Mary's University. When she's not writing, she likes to scuba dive, forget to go to kickboxing class, wallow in bed with a good book or get out her new guitar with a group of friends and pretend she's Suzanne Vega.

She loves to hear from readers—e-mail TracyMontoya@aol.com or visit www.tracymontoya.com.

Books by Tracy Montoya

HARLEQUIN INTRIGUE
750—MAXIMUM SECURITY
877—HOUSE OF SECRETS*
883—NEXT OF KIN*
889—SHADOW GUARDIAN*
986—FINDING HIS CHILD
1032—TELLING SECRETS

*Mission: Family

CAST OF CHARACTERS

Alex Gray—A search-and-rescue tracker for Renegade Ridge State Park.

Sophie Brennan—Sophie has had psychic impulses since she was a child, but her talent is uncontrollable, unreliable and subject to vanishing whenever she feels pressured.

Anna Gray—Alex's mother left the Pine Woods Reservation with her son after her husband murdered its tribal president.

Jack Runningwater—Alex's father and Anna's ex-husband. A fugitive from the law for over two decades, Jack may be behind a new series of killings in Port Renegade.

Jonathan Wainwright—The CEO of the Centrix Chemical Corporation has some secrets of his own—and they're tied to the Oglala and the Runningwaters.

Robert Felden—Wainwright's "left hand" hides in the shadows and does his boss's bidding—whatever that may be.

Wilma Red Cloud—The first female tribal president of the Oglala Lakota on the Pine Woods Reservation. The story of Wilma's murder by Jack Runningwater has become part of contemporary American history.

Rebecca Red Cloud—Wilma Red Cloud's sister and current tribal president of Pine Woods.

Aaron Donovan—The Port Renegade police detective is investigating a bizarre string of murders disguised as cult killings.

Sabrina Adelante—Aaron's wife and Alex's search-and-rescue colleague.

Millie Price—Sophie's nosy neighbor.

Chapter One

Alex Gray didn't know the woman who was staring so intently at him from the far side of the Bagel & Bean coffee shop. All he knew was that she made him nervous, in a not-so-good kind of way.

"Sabrina," he murmured to his longtime tracking partner and fellow member of Port Renegade's Search and Rescue team. "You know her?" He indicated the woman with a slight tilt of his head—subtle, if he did say so himself.

Sabrina Adelante took her customary latte from the barista and turned toward the redhead seated several feet away from them. The woman swiftly jerked her head to look out the window, but not before Sabrina had seen her watching them.

"I don't." Sabrina took a careful sip of her latte and considered the woman over the lip of her cup. "But she seems to know you."

Swallowing his reflexive denial, Alex pretended to be absorbed in reading the specials on the chalkboard over the woman's head while he checked her out once again. She was pretty, in a non-knockout kind of way, her most standout feature being the brownish-red and undoubtedly natural curls that she'd piled atop her head. A few had escaped to frame her oval face, emphasizing a delicately pointed chin and a pair of large dark eyes. She may have had the looks to blend in with the crowd, but he had to admit, there was also something about her, something that made him sure he would have remembered her if they'd met before. Especially those eyes—when she'd been staring at him, it was as if she knew…everything, all of his secrets, his darkest thoughts, down to the bone.

Her head swung around, and he was caught again by her dark gaze. This time, she didn't look away.

"Ah, crap." Alex spun around and headed for the door. Anything to get away from that too-intense woman, because he wasn't sure he wanted to find out why she was so fascinated with him. That definitely wasn't a casual "hey, you're kinda hot" stare, and anything else probably meant trouble.

Sabrina pushed out the door a few seconds later, her hands wrapped protectively around her latte, likely trying to leach warmth out of the cup as the cold air hit her. Port Renegade, Washington, never got all that much sun, but the November day was even grayer than usual, with the sharp biting feel of an impending storm in the air. "So what was that all about? Should I be on the lookout for some guy with a shotgun who wants you to make an honest woman out of his daughter?"

He raised one gloved hand, the stiff outer fabric of his waterproof parka making swishing sounds as he moved. "Swear to God, I've never seen her before in my life."

Sabrina took a careful sip of her coffee while glancing back toward the shop. "Well, better start running, Casanova, because she's coming outside." She leaned forward, straining to see through the gray-sky glare on the shop's front windows. "And she looks seriously unhappy."

A smattering of snowflakes started to fall, the light, airy kind that looped and danced in the air like miniature pixies before they finally hit the ground. Alex watched them as he curled his toes into the cushioned soles of his hiking boots and quashed the urge to bolt. Whatever she wanted, he'd let her have her say, and then they could both move on. Even with his obscured view of her through the glass double doors, he could see she wasn't much over five feet tall. He could take her.

Another Bagel & Bean customer strode past him, a little too closely, and Alex shifted his weight to avoid getting pushed over. The man yanked the door open, and there she stood, still aiming that scary-intense look right at Alex. She didn't even seem to notice when the man jostled past her, obviously feeling an urgent need to get some caffeine into his system.

She wasn't rail thin—probably about a size twelve or fourteen—but she had the most amazingly small waist, emphasized by a fitted green sweater, from which her generous hips flared in a way that practically invited a man to put his hands on them and hold on. As the door closed behind her, Alex could see she'd left her coat hanging on the chair she'd just vacated. But that didn't stop her from heading his way, an expression of firm resolve on her face, acting as if the cold didn't bother her in the least.

Once she got within a couple feet of him, however, she planted her boots on the wet cement walkway and sucked in her cheeks, her expression morphing into something less confident. In fact, it was almost a wince, as if she expected him to get angry at her mere presence. But why the hell would he be angry? He'd told Sabrina he'd never met this woman before, and up close and personal, he was still positive that was true. But the way she reacted to him threw him, all the same.

They stared at each other for what seemed like a very long time, playing a strange mental game of chicken. Naturally competitive, Alex dug his heels in and refused to be the first one to speak. Behind him, Sabrina muttered something under her breath, and he heard her hiking boots clunk across the pavement as she moved a polite distance away. When the silence had stretched out for too long, his natural concern drove him to finally break it. "Are you okay?"

Her hand floated up to toy with the neckline of her sweater. She had the most perfectly shaped rosebud of a mouth, dotted with the occasional freckle like the rest of her pale skin, and it turned upward in a small self-deprecating smile. "Sorry. I just—" Covering her mouth, she cleared her throat. "Are you a tracker?"

Lacing his gloved fingers together, he cracked his knuckles, buying some time before he answered. Sabrina and he were on Renegade Ridge State Park's lead search and rescue team, a group that had gotten lots of media attention locally and nationally both for their rare dedication to old-fashioned footprint tracking and the resulting successful searches for lost hikers. He loved his job, and it wasn't beneath him to play up the details of what he did to try to impress a woman here and there. But he never knew how to react when people seemed overly starstruck by the idea—something that tended to happen when the local cable access channel reran the series of interviews they'd done with the trackers a little over a year earlier. "I—"

"Do you find missing people?" The intense look was back, telling him she definitely wasn't an admirer.

"Yes," he replied. "You didn't lose someone in the park recently, did you?"

"No."

The tension that had suddenly built up in his body drained away at her denial, leaving him feeling half relieved that there wasn't a lost hiker in need of rescue and half disappointed that he wasn't going to get called in on a search this morning.

But though he waited, she didn't volunteer any further information, instead becoming strangely preoccupied with tracing the square toe of her impractical, clunky black boot along a crack in the sidewalk. Living in the mountains and doing what he did for a living, he'd made it a habit never to go out without a pair of shoes he could run and climb in. With that gigantic heel on hers, he wondered how she could even walk.

"Okay, do I know you?" he tried again.

"No. Not even slightly," she said to her shoe.

"Thennnnnnn, can you tell me what this is about?" This was like trying to get his ex-girlfriend Trina to tell him what he'd done to make her angry— on way too many occasions. Hence the whole ex-girlfriend thing. This woman didn't look like a drama queen like Trina, but you just never knew....

"There's a trail you'll be on today," she blurted out suddenly. "It's beautiful—runs by a two-tiered waterfall with a small fence at the bottom where the water pools and a really tall pine tree on the far side." She finally made eye contact with him, making circular motions with her hands. "The path there makes a loop."

Her eyes were pretty, a deep, dark blue, not brown as he'd originally thought, which reminded him of the ocea— *Focus, dude.* "Sounds like

Dungeness Falls." He cleared his throat and focused.

"Okay." Her eyes flicked to the ground and back up at him. "Don't take the kids to the far side of the water."

"What?"

"Don't take the kids to the far side of the water." She ducked her head again and mumbled, "Don't ask me how I know that." After imparting that strange bit of wisdom, she pivoted back toward the coffee shop, obviously wanting to make a quick escape. He stopped her by grabbing her elbow— gently, so as not to scare her, but firmly enough to keep her from bolting.

"What does that mean?" he asked. "What kids?"

"Generally speaking, all of this will make sense later." The strange half smile was back. "Unless I'm wrong, and then it'll just be embarrassing. But right now, that's all I can tell you."

"I don't have kids." Frustration and confusion warred for dominance inside him, and he tight- ened his grip on her arm. She probably was a drama queen after all, what with the cryptic messages and the big, pretty, I'm-so-lonely-come- save-me eyes. And all he knew was that he needed to stay far, far away from that type. History showed that he didn't do well with drama queens. "And could you please make sense for maybe five minutes? How do you know who I am? What kind of message is that?"

Now the smile was gone, replaced with the look of someone who'd had her puppy kicked too many times, which made him feel like a huge jerk. But then again, that was what drama queens did. They manipulated you into feeling sorry for them, and then—BAM! They hit you while you were vulnerable, just so they could fight and make up.

But instead of hitting him, literally or figuratively, she reached down and calmly peeled his hand off her elbow. "Trust me, you don't want to know." With that, she headed back inside the coffee shop, leaving him to wonder at her bizarro-world way of holding a conversation. Pulling his Mariners ball cap out of one of his jacket's oversize pockets, he jammed it backward over his head and turned toward his truck, hoping that getting her out of his sight would exorcise her from his brain.

But, of course, he had no such luck. As he slogged across the parking lot to where Sabrina was waiting for him, he found that any attempt to turn his thoughts away from the woman, her strange words and her cartoon-character eyes proved futile. She'd gotten stuck in his craw, and he wanted her out of his craw and as far, far away from it as possible.

Sabrina reached over and opened the driver's-side door for him, making a big show of shivering and chattering her teeth once he'd gotten inside.

"Sorry. I know you're cold." He got in and started the truck, cranking the defrost to clear the windows, which were nearly covered by a thin layer of moisture.

"I thought you might be a while, so I got your coffee." As soon as she'd handed him the small paper cup she'd been holding, she rubbed her bare hands vigorously together, then replaced her gloves. "By the way, you are so going to hate me."

"Okay, enough with the mysterious commentary. Just tell me straight what's going on." It took a major effort not to snap at her after she'd been nice enough to get the drink he'd forgotten, but his words still came out sharper than he'd intended.

Sabrina reared back in surprise. "Whoa, Mr. Grumpy Pants, who tied your boxers in a knot this morning?"

He sighed, leaning back in his seat and taking a sip of his coffee, which was already lukewarm from waiting in the frozen truck. Of course, Sabrina had also probably sucked all the heat out of it with her perpetually icy hands while he'd entertained the crazy woman in the parking lot. "Nothing." He made an effort to bring his voice back to a normal conversational tone. "So why am I going to hate you?"

She tried to smile at him, but it quickly turned to a toothy grimace, as if she expected him to start shouting at her once he figured out what the hell *she* was talking about. "Because I forgot to tell you that we have a bunch of fifth graders coming out to the park today to learn about tracking, and you get to take them on a hike."

"Excuse me, your what hurts?" he asked calmly.

Sabrina completely ignored the sarcastic non

sequitur. "I'm sorry, Al, but Jessie is mapping out the road closures for the winter with Skylar, and I promised Aaron I'd take Rosie in to the doctor today. She has a virus she can't shake." Aaron was Sabrina's new husband of six months, and Rosie was his teenaged daughter—who, come to think of it, hadn't been coming around to watch her step-mother work as often as usual lately. The girl was fascinated with tracking.

"She okay?"

"Yeah, just a fever and a nasty cough. We think it might be bronchitis, but I don't want to put off taking her in."

The truck finally warmed up, and he took that as a cue to turn on the windshield wipers to finish clearing the windshield. "No, don't do that. I can take the kids around, no problem."

That earned him a real smile from Sabrina as she clicked her seat belt into place. "You are fabulous, and I adore you."

"I know, but we must never speak of this again. Aaron would be mad at me, and I might have to kick his ass to defend myself," he said, referring to her husband, a police detective and good friend.

"Right." Sabrina laughed, holding her gloved hands in front of the heater vent. "Poor kids, they probably didn't expect snow today. Well, as you know, they'll want a demonstration from the big, bad search-and-rescue tracker, so I left some footprints last night down by Dungeness Falls for you to read for them."

He froze, his coffee cup floating a couple of millimeters from his mouth. "Say that again."

"I left some tracks down by Dungeness Falls." Narrowing her eyes, Sabrina pivoted in her seat to face him, reaching back to pull her long black ponytail over her shoulder so she could finger the ends. "Alex, you've been acting really stran—"

He didn't wait to hear the rest of her sentence, instead bolting out of the truck and heading for the shop. His breath coming out in heavy puffs from the cold, he shoved through the doors, barely noticing as he clipped a heavyset man balancing a cardboard tray filled with steaming cups in both hands. The man grunted a "Hey!" at him, but Alex just muttered an apology and kept moving, darting around the closely set tables to the one in the back where she'd been sitting.

She was gone. Jacket, coffee cup, all gone.

Don't take the kids to the far side of the water.

She'd known. She'd known he was headed to Dungeness Falls today, and she'd known about the kids on the field trip before he had. He pushed back through the shop and headed toward the parking lot once more, nearly upsetting the same Weeble-shaped man he'd almost toppled a few minutes earlier—dude sure didn't move fast. Once outside, he searched like a madman among the cars sitting in the small parking lot, looking for signs of telltale curls or a too-intense stare as he ignored Sabrina's shouted questions. But the woman wasn't there anymore. And he didn't even know her name.

Smacking his palm against the nearest car hood, Alex blew out a frustrated breath, still scanning the parking lot, even though he now knew it was a hopeless cause. He'd just spotted the footprints her ridiculous clunky boots had made in the thin layer of snow that now coated the ground, and they led to a parking spot that was now empty.

Don't take the kids to the far side of the water.

What the hell was he supposed to do now?

Chapter Two

"So even though it's snowing, you can still see a slight depression in the snow where our mystery woman left tracks," Alex called out over an excited group of fifth graders. About ten of them hung on his every word, bumping heads every time they bent down to see something he had to show them on the ground. The rest were pretty much touch and go—sometimes he captured their interest, and other times they got distracted by something shiny. But all in all, they were a pretty decent group of kids. He liked fifth grade—they were old enough to have an interesting conversation with, but still young enough to be dazzled by his tracking brilliance. Not that he'd tell Sabrina that—she still thought he was doing her a giant favor.

He started walking backward, beckoning to the group to follow him. "Here you'll notice our subject started veering off the path." He gestured toward a smattering of tall grasses, some of which were bent and broken. "Plants don't crush themselves, so you can see something's been here. Since the footprints we're following seem to have disappeared off the path, looking for broken vegetation is the next best thing."

"Oooh, that's so cool!" said one gum-chomping girl as she pushed her trendy red glasses up higher on her nose, smiling brightly.

He laughed softly. "Be careful. That's how I got into this business—I thought tracking was cool. But it's also exhausting and sometimes cold, wet and nasty."

"But you get to save lives. That's awesome," she responded.

True. And that was the best part, finding lost hikers and bringing them home.

"Are you Native American?" a boy bundled in a puffy purple jacket and a Minnesota Vikings stocking hat interjected. His voice was partially muffled by the yellow-and-purple scarf someone had wrapped around the lower half of his face, dark brown eyes peering over it. It wasn't *that* cold, but some parents couldn't be too careful when it came to their children.

"Yes." *Don't say it. Don't say it. Don't say it.* Alex's teeth clicked together in an involuntary jaw clench as he waited for the inevitable question.

The boy pulled the scarf off his face, clumsily, as his hands were encased in some hard-core ski mittens. Alex felt the tension leave his shoulders when he noticed that the boy's skin was slightly tanner than that of the Caucasian children in his class. "I'm Ojibwa, from Minnesota. We're not trackers. Is your tribe?"

"Thank you. I have a lot of people assume that I'm a tracker because of some mysterious Native American power." He smiled at the boy, who grinned back in understanding. "I'm Oglala Lakota Sioux, but I grew up off the reservation. And no, the Sioux aren't trackers, to my knowledge." He'd been six when his mother had moved off the reservation with her only child, so he didn't actually know a whole lot about the Lakota except for the few things Anna Gray had told him through the years.

The girl with the glasses raised her hand, so high and straight above her head, her tummy stuck out with the effort.

"Yes?" Alex waved at her so she'd feel free to ask her question.

"Where did you learn to track, then?" Her hand remained in the air, even though he'd already called on her.

"I took a class as a college student from the park rangers here to fulfill a phys ed requirement when I couldn't get into weight training, and I liked it so much, I designed my own semester abroad to Botswana to study tracking and desert survival with the Kalahari San." At their puzzled looks, he added, "You might know them as the Bushmen. They're tribal people in Africa, and their tracking skills are legendary. As luck would have it, the group who took me in were also brilliant teachers. I came back here to do a mountain-tracking apprenticeship, and they hired me."

After fielding a few questions about his Africa experience and telling them how he learned to always keep his tent zipped in the Kalahari—to keep the hyenas out—Alex headed down the trail once more, showing them how to spot the sign indicating where his coworker's trail continued.

It wasn't until he heard water rushing through rocks that he felt the first pangs of uneasiness.

Don't take the kids to the far side of the water.

But that was where the trail led. Across the water. And a successful field trip meant following the tracks around the entire Dungeness Falls loop, at the end of which one of the park rangers would be waiting with a picnic lunch to tell them about Renegade Ridge's history and point out some interesting sights.

What had she been warning him about? Should he just ignore her? Was she an overprotective parent who'd decided to be spooky and weird about her fear of having her child near water? Was she insane?

Maybe she was insane. An insane bomber who had rigged the bridge over the falls to explode once they set foot on it.

Ah, hell. Now *he* was being insane. But he also couldn't just ignore her. If any of the kids under his watch got hurt because he ignored Ms. Batcrap-crazy's warning, he'd regret it for the rest of his life. He should have just called the police and had them sort this out, but now it was too late. He was in charge of a group of thirty-odd fifth graders, and he alone had to decide whether they were going to cross the water in about fifteen minutes.

Pulling the radio off his belt, he brought it up to his mouth. "Hey, kids, here's how we communicate with the ranger station during a scarch," he said brightly. Probably too brightly, judging from the confused look one of the chaperones had just shot him. Toning down his *Mister Rogers' Neighbor-hood* smile, he depressed the talk button with his thumb. "Base, this is tracker one-B, over."

A burst of static, and then came, "Roger that, tracker one-B, how can we help you, over?"

"I need you to patch me over to Sabrina's cell phone, over." He hoped that Sabrina, who had set the tracks he and the schoolkids were following, had taken her phone with her on the way to her step-daughter's appointment.

"Hey, Al, what's up?" Sabrina asked, never hav-ing been one for radio protocol via cell phone. "Uh, over."

"Bree, I'm just about to cross Dungeness Falls. Did you see anything strange up here when you were laying these tracks last night, over?" Natu-rally, none of the kids were distracted at the moment, and all were hanging on his every word.

Thirty pairs of eyes widened when he asked about "anything strange," and then the kids started whispering excitedly among themselves. Great. Now he'd scared them all. Their parents would be overjoyed.

"No, Al. Everything was pretty normal. What in particular are you looking for, over?" she responded.

"Nothing. Never mind." Without so much as an *over,* he clicked off the radio and returned it to his belt. "Okay," he said to the kids, "let's head around this bend to the falls, and you can all stop and take pictures if you want." He didn't know how many of them, if any, would have cameras, but he figured that sounded plausible. While they were resting, he'd head up the trail next to the falls and check out the far side of the bridge. And if he saw anything remotely threatening, this was going to be the world's shortest field trip.

After leading the students to the lookout point near the falls, he told them to fan out so they could all see the spectacular rush of white water as it plunged down a steep, rocky incline to spray into a pool at the bottom. The falls weren't particularly tall—maybe twenty feet or so—but they were beautiful.

Reaching across the fence to run his palm through the cloud of fine, cool mist at the foot of the falls, he scanned the crowd to make sure they were all busy oohing and aahing. Then, after a word to one of their teachers, he headed up the trail. With long, quick strides, he made short work of the switchbacks leading to the top of the falls, then jogged along the path beside the upper part of the Dungeness River until he reached a small wooden bridge.

Don't take the kids to the far side of the water.

Resting a hand on the smoothly sanded pine of the guardrail, he looked across. The path curved just a few feet after the bridge into a dense stand of Sitkas, dripping moss and low-hanging branches obscuring his view. Whatever it was that the mystery woman had wanted him to keep the kids away from, he couldn't see it from this side. So, did her message mean that it was all right for him to go across the water alone?

Curiosity. One of these days, it was going to get him killed. But today, he didn't figure that a cryptic message from a strange curly-haired woman was going to accomplish that feat. He made his way to the other side of the gurgling stream of water and thumped his boot emphatically on the dirt path once he reached the other side, mentally daring said curly-haired woman to come and get him.

She didn't. So he kept going.

A few minutes later, something large and white—a bright, pristine white that didn't occur naturally in the forest—caught his eye a few yards off the path.

"She probably left you a body, champ," he muttered under his breath. "You think she's cute.

Therefore, she must be a wack-job." For some reason, he'd always been like a magnet for that type, and it was starting to get old.

Small twigs and leaves crackled under his feet as he left the path and made his way through the undergrowth. Batting a low-hanging branch out of his way, he squinted at the white object, hoping its brilliance would suddenly make sense, that its presence would be something perfectly innocuous.

He pushed through the last of the tall weeds and bristly shrubs in his way, and the thing was finally visible. And what he saw there chilled him to the bone.

"Holy—"

Backing away slowly, Alex pulled his radio off his belt once more. "Base, this is tracker one-B, over."

"Tracker one-B, this is Base. What's your twenty, over?"

"About one hundred yards above the falls on Dungeness." He was nearly overcome by an overwhelming urge to get out of there as quickly as possible. That or throw up. But he had a job to do, and no one else was up here to do it. "I need you to call the police, and get every park ranger you've got to block off this trail." He scrubbed a hand over his face, still unable to believe what his eyes were telling him.

"Alex, are you okay?" Skylar, the search-and-rescue coordinator slipped out of her usual radio-speak. He'd blocked off trails before, for less grisly reasons, but she'd obviously become alarmed at something she heard in his voice.

"Yeah, just—" He took a deep breath. "Skylar, I've never seen anything like this. Just call the police. I've got to get those kids away from here."

Chapter Three

"Authorities are seeking this woman, wanted for questioning…"

Sophie Brennan jerked forward in her seat when she saw the composite drawing flash up on her television, which then sent her fumbling in between the couch cushions for the remote. Once her hand closed on the thing, she hit the button to turn up the volume, not taking her eyes off the face on the screen.

Her face.

"…in a bizarre murder that witnesses say could have been the work of a satanic cult."

Okay, now *that* she hadn't seen coming.

Her phone started ringing, but she just turned the volume up even higher, deciding to let the machine answer the call.

"The name of the victim and cause of death have not been released by the Port Renegade Police," the newscaster said cheerily from her position off-camera, Sophie's face still getting more than its share of screen time. "But a police spokesperson did confirm that the body was discovered around 9:30 this morning by a search-and-rescue worker for Renegade Ridge State Park."

Sophie leaned toward the TV and squinted at her likeness. The nose was wrong, but other than that, they'd pretty much hit the mark. Which meant that her busybody neighbors were probably going to start calling the sheriff's office any minute. God, someone had *died.* You'd think she would've known that.

"One witness who asked to remain anonymous said the body was covered by a white sheet and had been stabbed in the chest in a circle-and-cross pattern. Sources say the wounds were consistent with ritual murders." Finally, the news channel took that awful drawing off the air, focusing on the newscaster's face, which was framed by a bright blond helmet of hair. "Expert Marvin Wynter, author of *Free Your Mind! Deprogramming Former Cult Members,* is here to talk to us," the reporter said. "Marvin, could this be the work of cult killers?"

The camera cut to a man in his fifties, with shifty little eyes and a thick beard. "Why, yes, all of the signs are there—"

Not waiting to hear the so-called expert pontificate further, Sophie hit the mute button. One didn't need to be psychic to see that the guy was nothing but a fearmonger.

But as for the rest of the broadcast... She sat back against the couch cushions and grabbed a throw pillow to hug to her chest, trying to process what she'd just seen. She hadn't thought for a minute that her warning to Alex Gray, search-and-rescue tracker extraordinaire, would result in a police sketch of her plastered on the evening news. And in her wildest dreams she hadn't thought it would lead to a murder victim.

But it did, and it had. So now what?

Her pulse pounding in triple-time, she realized that the most rational option was to turn herself in to the police before someone else did—if she still had time. A Ph.D. candidate in art history at the University of Washington–Port Renegade, Sophie was pretty much the stereotypical impoverished grad student, so she lived in an inexpensive but nice and secure apartment complex to save money. Unfortunately, the reason that said apartment complex was such a steal when it came to rent was that it catered to an elderly clientele, and anyone under the age of retirement seemed to stay far, far away from it. So while that meant she could tap into the considerable wisdom of her elders just by wandering down the hall to see who was using the fitness room, it also meant that she was surrounded by more than her share of ladies and gentlemen of leisure who were bored out of their minds—and filled in the gaps in their daily schedules by keeping close watch on the goings-on around them. She'd bet the Port Renegade PD had had at least fifty calls from her neighbors ratting her out in the last five minutes alone, bless their hearts.

Okay, so she could wait for the police to come to her, she could go to them, or…

Or. She could go find Alex Gray and explain herself. After their meeting, she'd found it easy enough to unearth information about him—he'd been involved in so many public rescues of hikers lost in the state park, his picture was plastered across several issues of the *Port Renegade Tribune-Herald's* online archive. Finding his house would be a snap.

Now there was a brilliant idea. She'd already weirded him out in a big bad way this morning at the Bagel & Bean. If she approached him again, he'd probably either run away screaming or have her arrested on stalking charges as well as brought in for questioning. Surely going to find Alex Gray had to be one of her worst contingency plans ever.

Then why wouldn't the idea leave her alone?

She was saved from answering that question for herself when the phone rang again. She got up and padded in her stocking feet to the kitchen area of her apartment, where her phone sat. A glance at the caller ID told her it was her mom, and as much as she loved her mother, she just couldn't deal with her right now, so she let the machine pick up.

"Sophie?" her mother's voice rang out in the silent kitchen. "Sophie, why aren't you answering my calls? I know you're there—you're screening me again, aren't you? Sophie, your face was on the evening news. The police want you brought in for questioning! Sophie, what's going on? Are you okay? Call your mother once in a while, all right? I'd like to know why my kid is being questioned about a murder. I'm so worried about you. Okay. Call me. I don't know why you don't carry a cell phone—" *Beep!*

Finally, blessedly, the machine cut her mother off. Sophie touched a button to erase the message and headed for her front door. If she didn't get out of here, guilt would eat her alive until she called her mom back, and she didn't want to do that until she'd gotten herself out of this mess. Kate Brennan worried enough as it was.

Pulling her black midlength leather jacket on, she zipped it up and wrapped a long scarf around her neck. Where to—police, Alex Gray or undisclosed hidden location? Undisclosed hidden location, Alex Gray or police?

Grabbing her keys off the little hook near the door, she peered through the peephole to make sure no one was lurking in the hall. Reasonably confident that she could make it to the stairwell to the parking garage without being accosted, she exited her apartment, locking the door behind her. A leaden weight seemed to settle in the bottom of her stomach, reminding her that for better or worse, she was inextricably tied to a murder. And what she did now could help the investigation or throw it way off track—or get her in some serious trouble.

Maybe she was in serious trouble no matter what she did.

TRY AS HE MIGHT, ALEX COULDN'T erase the disturbing sight of that sheet-covered…thing from his mind, no matter how many times Sabrina and Skylar asked if he was all right, no matter how many mindless *South Park* reruns he went over in his head, no matter how many times he closed his eyes.

He'd been inside the ranger station since the morning, after he'd gotten the schoolkids safely back on their bus without them being any wiser. He'd told their teachers he'd seen a bear, and the field-trip chaperones had been only too happy to clear on out rather than risk having one of their charges eaten by errant wildlife. And then, after leading the police to the body, he'd come back to the station and had answered questions: Sabrina's questions, Skylar's questions, the park rangers' questions, the police detectives' questions. Over and over and over again, further embedding the images in his brain. And they were horrific.

When he'd gone up the falls, he'd found a body. But not just a lost hiker or a suicide, as was usually the case on the rare occasions when someone died in the parklands. No, this person had most definitely been murdered, but unfortunately, the killer hadn't left it at that.

Somewhere between the hours of 6:00 last night and 9:30 this morning, someone had constructed a stone altar, laid the body on it and covered it with a sheet. Then, just to make things nice and scary for the poor schmo who ended up finding the victim, they'd stabbed an upside-down cross pattern through the sheet and into the victim's chest. The cops Alex had led to the scene had told him that the stab wounds had been inflicted postmortem and that the victim had most likely been strangled, but if that was supposed to make him feel better, it didn't.

The police had long ago finished gathering evidence from the scene, and even though it was past time for him to go home for the day, Alex remained inside one of the ranger station offices, sitting at a desk with his head in his hands, waiting to see if he could be of any more use to…anyone. Anything rather than go home and be alone with his thoughts.

Someone had died. Within a mile of the ranger station, and no one had heard or seen or suspected a thing.

No one except the woman he'd met outside the coffee shop that morning.

He'd given her description to police, and they'd said they'd put an APB out on her to bring her in for questioning. Had he met a murderer? And if so, didn't it just figure that she'd randomly choose to torment *him* with clues about her crimes?

A knock at the door brought him out of his thoughts. "Come in," he called, and Sabrina popped her head through the door.

"Alex, there's a woman wearing a very large pair of sunglasses outside. She's asking to speak to you." Sabrina narrowed her eyes, glancing quickly behind her. "I think it's that woman from the coffee shop."

Of course. Right on cue.

Feeling more exhausted than he could remember, he planted his hands on the desk and pushed himself wearily to his feet. "Seriously? You call the police?"

She nodded. "Of course. I don't want to lose her, but what if she's dangerous? Maybe you shouldn't go out there."

"If she's that dangerous, she would have come in here, guns blazing." Then again, the murder victim had been a healthy male in his fifties who'd outweighed her by at least a hundred pounds. If she'd managed to take him down, she might be more formidable than she looked. The thought didn't stop him from heading for the door. "I'll stall her," he said to Sabrina. "You tell the cops to hurry." Someone had to keep her occupied until the police arrived, and he wasn't going to send out Skylar or Bree and cower behind them.

He pushed through the ranger-station doors and headed outside. In the dimness of the parking lot lights, he could barely make out a lone figure standing next to a small gray compact car, a fringed scarf wrapped around her hair. Just as Sabrina had told him, she wore a pair of sunglasses so huge, they looked like they'd eaten half her face. As he approached, she got in her car, leaning over to open the passenger-side door in an obvious invitation.

Once he'd climbed inside, pausing briefly to scan the interior and make sure she didn't have a tranq gun hidden on the floor somewhere, she unwrapped the scarf from around her head and took off the ridiculous sunglasses. And yes, indeed, it was her—the woman from the coffee shop. The insane woman from the coffee shop whose bizarre message had led him to the body of someone who'd died in a way that no one should.

"What do you want?" His words were harsh, and he didn't feel the least bit sorry for her when she flinched at his tone.

She licked her lips, and he was close enough to her to see the light dusting of freckles on her face. The curls that he'd thought were mostly brown had taken on a fiery reddish hue in the light of the setting sun. "My name is Sophie Brennan, and I wanted to apologize," she began. "I had no idea what I told you this morning would lead you to…what you found." She shifted her weight slightly in her seat, so she was leaning away from him as if she were afraid. He scowled at the thought that he would have frightened her—*he* wasn't the one sending people to find murder victims.

"What I found was a body," he said, trying to keep himself from shouting at her. "And you knew something was there, across the bridge. You mind telling me how?"

"I don't—" She flipped her palms upward, blinked a couple of times and then let her hands drop to her lap once more.

"Look," Alex said, trying another tactic. "My coworker's husband is a cop. He can help you, if you just tell us what you know." He didn't know why he'd offered her even that much protection. But then again, now that he was face-to-face with her, it was difficult to picture her as the one who'd performed that grisly killing. This quiet, somewhat shy woman with her too-intense eyes didn't seem like the type to murder someone and then carry out some bizarre ritual with their remains. Plus, the victim had been a big man, and she barely cleared five feet. Strangulation? He didn't think so.

Or so his gut told him. Then again, lots of people's guts had told them Ted Bundy was an okay guy, before the whole being-outed-as-a-serial-killer thing had happened.

She shook her head emphatically. "I don't need help. They won't find any evidence on or near the body that ties it to me, because I had nothing to do with that murder." Folding her arms, she looked him straight in the eye then, her deep blue gaze solid and seemingly filled with the naive belief that her proven innocence was a sure thing. "Look." She took a deep breath, then continued. "I'm a little psychic. That was why I talked to you at the coffee shop."

"You're a little what?" Now that he hadn't seen coming. "How can you be a little psychic? Isn't that like being a little rich, or a little dead?"

She gave something between a snort and a laugh. "Not in my case." With that, she pulled off the leather gloves she wore, squeezing them in one of her now-bare hands. "Basically, I'm a really bad psychic."

Now it was his turn to laugh.

"I don't get visions, I don't see dead people, I don't even hear little voices in my head," she continued. "But sometimes, I just get this big, nagging sense that I have to say something or do something. It doesn't seem to come from anywhere in particular, but it's like an itch I can't scratch." She stopped squeezing. "I saw you in the coffee shop, and I just had to talk to you."

He shook his head, opening his mouth to reply and finding that he had nothing to say to that.

"Ummmm…" She swallowed. "I mean, I felt like I had to tell you something. And when I finally got up the nerve to approach you, that thing about the kids and the water just came flying out." She fluttered one hand in front of her like a butterfly to illustrate, then pulled it back, curling both hands around her gloves so the leather squeaked slightly. "I had no idea if I was right about what I told you until I saw the news tonight."

"Great." It sounded so far-fetched, but something in him almost believed her. She seemed so sincere, so…*normal*. But there was nothing normal about a ritualistic murder in a state park. And there was nothing normal about warning someone not to take children near the place where a dead body waited. "You know the police think you might have something to do with that murder, right? And your defense is you're a psychic who sucks?" He leaned back in his seat, stretching his arm across the ridge between the door and the window. "Sweetheart, I don't have to have my own 1-900 line to know that that isn't going to get you very far."

"Then why haven't you called the police yet?"

Just then, a wailing siren sounded in the distance, growing louder with every passing second. Oh, yeah, if she was what she said she was, she sure had the "who sucks" part down if she hadn't seen that one coming.

"You did call them. Before you even got in the car." She dropped her gloves and whirled around, clutching at the door handle and looking very much like a trapped rabbit—soft, scared and completely clueless as to what to do next. "I'm such an idiot."

A police car careened into the parking lot, lights flashing, only to be followed by another. And another.

Several more skidded to a halt around the parking-lot exit, forming a haphazard line that would prevent any cars from going in or out. Their respective sirens blended together into one shrieking, cacophonous alarm, somewhat muffled inside the closed doors of the car.

"I didn't think I warranted this much effort," she shouted at him.

"Get out of the car, and put your hands in the air!" a tinny voice outside blared through a bullhorn.

She yanked the keys out of her car ignition and shoved them in her pocket. "You slept with a woman named Penny last month," she said suddenly to the windshield.

"Wha—" How could she know that? Penny lived in another state and had claimed to have no friends in Washington when she'd visited on business.

"She has a blog, and she's very, very peeved at you." Sophie sighed, and her shoulders dropped in defeat. She switched off the car's headlights. "See? I'm awful. I wish I could throw some secret or something that only you and your dead aunt Polly know at you, but I can't. All I know is that when it's really, really important, sometimes words come to me that are meaningful to someone else. I'm not a murderer." She opened the car door and raised her hands as she got ready to exit the vehicle.

"And I don't know why, but I'll see you again," she shouted over the noise that had grown significantly louder since she'd opened the door. "This murder is connected to you in more ways than you know. And I think I have to help you with something." She rolled her eyes, her body half in, half out of the car. "Although why I would help a guy who thinks I'm a satanic cult killer is beyond me."

With that, she got out, heading for the cops waiting for her with her head held high, and leaving him to wonder at the strength of her seemingly unshakable conviction in her innocence.

And how, with a seemingly random comment, she could have hit on the fact that he had a dead aunt Polly.

Chapter Four

Alex's stomach rumbled as he pulled his pickup into his driveway, an insistent reminder that it was well past dinnertime. Good thing he'd stopped on the way to get a sandwich, or he might have wasted away to nothing trying to conjure up a meal out of a half-eaten bag of Fritos and a case of beer. If memory served, he'd been putting off grocery shopping for too long.

The police had questioned him only briefly about his conversation with Sophie Brennan, but somehow, time had gotten away from him as he'd filled in his coworkers, who'd all wanted to know the latest on why one woman warranted a major sting operation.

All signs pointed to the fact that said woman was somehow connected to the grisliest homicide Port Renegade had seen in decades. But murder? Ritual killings? He wasn't a go-with-your-gut kind of guy, preferring to deal with hard evidence, like footprints and broken plants. But from the little he'd observed of Sophie, he didn't think she had it in her.

Trouble was, he believed her story about being psychic about as much as he believed that little green men were going to visit him tonight and take him into space for sinister experiments.

Grabbing the slender plastic bag containing his sandwich and chips off the passenger seat, he exited the truck and retrieved his mail from the squeaky outdoor box next to his driveway, shoving the few thin envelopes and solicitation postcards into the oversize right pocket of his parka before heading for his front steps.

A few years back, through some hard-core savings and wise investments, Alex had managed to parlay his park-employee salary into a down payment on a house in the mountains. The house itself was a butt-ugly three-story block of brown siding that looked like a Jawa sandcrawler from the original *Star Wars* film. But inside, it was a little piece of heaven, with cherry hardwood floors that seemed to glow from within and a huge stone fireplace to match an equally huge kitchen. The entire outer wall of the master bedroom was a series of windows that looked out on the snow-capped peaks of the Olympics. But what had really sold him was the sweet deck overlooking an enormous tree-lined backyard.

Trouble was he hadn't yet had time to get much

in the way of furniture, for the deck or the house, but one of these days, he'd fix that.

Once inside, he threw his jacket on the nearest milk crate and tossed his baseball cap and jacket after it. Shaking the sandwich out of its skinny bag, he sank gratefully into the one piece of quality furniture he did own—a dark brown recliner—which faced the love of his life—a fifty-two-inch wide-screen HDTV hooked up to stereo surround sound. A man had to have his priorities.

He kicked back his weight; the recliner's footrest popped up, and Alex had everything he needed in life—a dinner he hadn't made, a comfy chair and the sports update on channel seven. Actually, if he had telekinetic powers and could float a beer from the refrigerator to his tragically empty hand, life would be complete. Maybe he should ask Sophie Brennan if her Jedi powers extended to levitating objects….

Stop it. Thinking about Sophie Brennan was only going to get him into trouble. Big, fat, crazy-girlfriend trouble. Why he was a magnet for that type, he'd never know, but the sooner he forgot her, the better. No thinking about Sophie Brennan. No hitting on Sophie Brennan. No nothing on, near or around Sophie Brennan.

Although he had to wonder what was happening to her down at the station. Maybe he could just call—

With a hiss of disgust, Alex cut off that train of thought, concentrating instead on a search-and-rescue mission for his TV remote, which had apparently become lodged inside the chair somewhere. He'd managed to extract it and turn on *SportsCenter* when the doorbell rang.

And all he could hear in his head as he went to answer the door was the last thing Sophie Brennan had said to him: *I'll see you again. This murder is connected to you in more ways than you know.*

Displaying a superhuman amount of self-control, Alex opened the door, discovering not Sophie standing behind it, but Sabrina and her husband, Aaron. Bree hadn't changed out of the waterproof winter gear she'd worn to work, and Aaron still had on a suit, which told Alex that this couldn't be good.

Her arms wrapped tightly around her body, Sabrina glanced at the sandwich in his hand. "Oh, wow, you haven't gotten a chance to eat dinner yet? We're sorry to bother you so late, Alex."

He stepped back, inviting them in with a casual motion of his head. "You're not bothering me." He gestured to Sabrina to take the recliner and swung a chair from his dining-room set over for Aaron. Although he could have sat in one of the chairs, as well, Alex decided to choose between the worn bean bag squatting in front of the TV or one of the handy, all-purpose plastic milk crates that dotted the floor plan of his house—he opted for the latter, kicking it over a few inches into optimal conversational position. "Beer?" he asked them both, seeing as that was about all he had to offer them at the moment.

"Sure." Aaron shed his coat and draped it over the back of the chair before sitting down.

"None for me, thanks," Sabrina added.

Once Alex had returned with two cold Thomas Kempers from the fridge, he handed one to Aaron and sat down. "So, what's up? Not that I don't appreciate the visit, but you both look like this is more than a friendly house call."

Sabrina glanced at Aaron, who leaned forward, resting his elbows on his parted knees. "You're right, Al. I wanted to talk to you about the murder victim you found today."

Suddenly, Alex wished he'd chosen the bean bag—the mere mention of the day's events caused what had remained of his energy level to plummet, and he just wanted to sink into the bag's nubby softness and forget everything that had happened today. Including and especially the people in his living room, friends though they were. He reached up and rubbed one of his eyebrows. "My talking to your colleagues for more than my entire work shift didn't give you the information you needed?"

"Alex—" Sabrina began.

"Sorry." Just because he'd had a crappy day didn't mean he had to take it out on them. "I'm just tired. Hungry. And freaked out."

She moved up to the edge of the recliner, so she, too, was leaning toward him. The two of them looked like a pair of shrinks waiting for him to tell them about his childhood. "No, Alex. It's just…"

She flung her hands in the air and turned to Aaron, clearly growing exasperated. "Tell him."

Aaron took his cue. "The county medical examiner hasn't had a chance to look at the body yet, but from the look I got, it seems like our guy was killed with a garrote. No blows to the head, gunshots or anything that would handicap him—someone strong and stealthy came up behind him and slipped a cord around his neck."

Like he needed to hear that before he'd had a chance to finish his sandwich. Damn cops. "You think he might have been immobilized somehow? It did look like some sort of cult got a hold of him." Alex looked down at the floor, tracing the grooves between the wood planks with his gaze. Anything to avoid picturing what he'd seen that morning.

"Maybe. But we didn't see any ligature marks on his body. M.E. can tell us for sure." Aaron took a swig of his beer, then leaned back in his chair, resting one ankle on the opposite knee. "But as for it being a ritual murder, I don't think so."

"Pretty much all reports of satanic-cult murders in the U.S. have turned out to be something completely different," Sabrina chimed in. "There are no documented cases of a satanic cult murdering anyone, ever. Just lots of mass hysteria. There's a report that came out of SUNY–Buffalo awhile back that investigated nearly 12,500 instances of so-called satanic activity and concluded there was no evidence such cults even existed."

Alex narrowed his eyes at her.

She shrugged, a sheepish smile spreading across her face. "You learn some interesting things when you're married to a police detective."

"Ah." He took a drink of his beer. "But what about the stab wounds?"

"The cross and circle?" Aaron asked. "Inflicted postmortem, judging from the amount of blood. And they mimic a murder that took place in Ohio a couple of years ago—a priest was convicted of killing a nun, and he tried to make the murder look like a satanic killing. In this case, someone wasn't being that creative."

"But why?"

Sabrina started moving around in her seat, first tucking her legs under her, then shifting around until she was in a lotus position. She drummed the back of her right hand against her leg for a few seconds, and then her feet went back on the floor. And since he'd known the woman since they'd gone to high school together, he knew that her fight-or-flight mechanism was kicking in big-time. Whenever the going got tough, tough Sabrina got moving. And if she couldn't move, she'd dance around in place until she could move.

And from where he sat, she was moving like crazy right now.

He set his beer on the floor with a thud. "What?"

She examined her thumbnail, picking occasionally at the cuticle. "There's more about what the police found on the body. Besides the manner of death, the garrote, there was other thing that didn't match the Ohio murder."

He was really growing tired of this. "Garrote, sheet, stone altar, stab wounds. What else do I need to know?" He turned to Aaron, appealing to the man's sense of decency to put him out of his misery and just spit it out already. "You're my best friends, but I'm about to shake you both until one of you starts talking. What didn't match?"

"Something was placed in the victim's hand, probably by the killer," Aaron said quietly. "A crow feather."

Everything stopped. Time, his breathing, his heart. From far, far away, he could hear Sabrina talking to him but he couldn't make out what she was saying. Blindly, he reached for his beer bottle, and when his fingers touched the cool, slick surface, he closed his hand around it and brought it up, taking a long, long swig out of it. But even alcohol didn't dull the pain blooming in slow motion inside his chest.

He inhaled sharply, glad to find that his lungs were still working, and forced the world back into focus. "A crow feather?" He knew that the redundant question wasn't going to magically make them give him a different answer, the answer he was hoping for.

Something in his reaction had Sabrina on her feet. She crouched down beside him and put her hand on his arm. Then she nodded. "Just like when Wilma Red Cloud was killed."

Another time, another place. Another murder that had happened years ago, on a reservation in South Dakota. A murder that had changed his life and had nearly wrecked his mother.

He'd forgotten. He'd made himself forget. He and his mother never talked about that time—even when he was a kid and had tried to get her to talk about it, she'd refused. And she'd been right; some things were best left in the dark.

Until, that is, they forced themselves out into the open again.

Crow carrier.

Clutching the bottle, so slick with condensation it nearly slipped out of his fingers, Alex shook his head sharply. Focus, don't think. Just focus. Don't feel. "So you think this might be tied to…" *Say it.*

But he couldn't say it, so he just looked up at his friends, hoping they couldn't see that he was drowning.

Sabrina rubbed his arm, her eyes wide with something he didn't want to name. "Your father? Al, I'm so sorry, but that's exactly what we think."

"EXCUSE ME, CAN I HELP YOU?"

Alex clenched his teeth and stifled a groan as yet another elderly resident of the Sunnyside View Apartments tapped on his truck window. With the pad of her index finger still pressed against the glass, the woman peered inside, actually moving her head around in circles as she scanned the cab's interior.

According to Aaron, Sophie had been released hours ago because, as she'd predicted, the police had had no evidence to tie her to the murder in the park. So here Alex was, sitting outside her apartment complex, having gotten here on a crazy impulse with no plan as to how to get her to spill her guts. But she'd known about the body, and if she knew that, then she probably knew something about his father. Once he figured out the best way to approach her, he wasn't leaving until he'd gotten the information he needed.

But first, he had to get through Sophie's neighbors, who were all significantly older than she, and apparently took their personal security very seriously. At least five Sunnyside octogenarians had trundled out in the last ten minutes to ask him what it was he wanted, who he was there to see and how long he planned to wait before he went home. Now that resident number six had arrived, he knew he had to figure out his plan sooner rather than later. Obviously Sophie's neighbors weren't going to give him the five damned minutes of quiet he needed to calm down and get himself together.

He tried to smile at the woman outside his truck, but his face felt tight and uncooperative. "I'm just waiting for someone," he finally said, knowing full well that she wasn't going to just nod and walk away.

"Oh?" She clamped her hand around the top of the glass, so he couldn't roll it back up without crushing her knobby fingers. "Who are you waiting for?"

He clenched his fingers around the steering wheel, half-tempted to wrench the thing off, just for some kind of release. "Sophie."

"Sophie who?" She leaned in closer, her beady eyes and half of her gray perm filling up the space between the window glass and the top of his door.

"Sophie Brennan."

The woman seemed to consider that for a moment. "Sophie never has gentlemen callers, especially after nine o'clock. I'd know about it. What's your name? Where do you live? What makes you think she wants to see you this late? The poor girl has her weekend study group tomorrow morning, you know."

"Ma'am, I'm not a gentleman caller. I'm just—" He yanked the keys out of the ignition, pausing when he couldn't think of how to finish that last statement. What was he? And more importantly, why couldn't he have just walked up to Sophie's apartment right away, instead of lurking out here and rousting the blue-haired brigade? "Wait a minute. Who are you? Where do *you* live? Because you can't be building security."

"Millie Price. And I'm not going to tell you where I live." She backed away from the window, raising her chin—all the better to slant a superior look at him. "You might be a rapist."

Oh, for the love of— "I'm not a rapist, ma'am. I'm a park ranger." He sighed. "I'm here to talk to her about my father." There. Just enough personal information so that maybe the woman would sense she'd crossed a line and back off already.

"I'm going to need to see some ID."

He pushed the door open and jumped out of the truck cab, his boots crunching into the snow. She reared back, clearly affronted, then fished her hand into the pocket of her lumpy light blue winter coat. Pulling out a pair of reading glasses, she settled them on her face and tilted her head so she could peer over the rims at him. Was it his imagination, or was an old lady who dressed like a Smurf actually getting all up in his face?

"Ma'am, with all due respect, I'm not here to see you. I'm here to see Sophie," he said. "And unless flames start shooting out of her apartment or you hear screams from behind her door, the rest is none of your business." With that, he brushed past her and headed for the building's front gate.

He heard her scurry along close behind him. "I'll have you know your presence is every bit my business," she huffed. "I'm the Sunnyside Neighborhood Watch captain, and you, sir, are a loiterer."

He felt a hand clutch at his parka. Mustering up the last of his patience, he turned to face her. "Look, Torquemada—"

"It's okay, Mrs. Price," a soft voice interrupted from a few feet away. And when Alex looked up,

Sophie Brennan was standing underneath a nearby streetlight, her arms crossed over her chest against the cold night air. Again, she wasn't wearing a coat, and instead of the clunky black shoes she'd had on earlier that day, she wore a pair of thick suede and cork Birkenstock sandals over her socks. Her face looked flushed and her eyelids heavy with sleep, as if she'd just tumbled out of bed and directly into the parking lot, pausing only to slip on yet another pair of inappropriate footgear. "I know him. Your work here is done."

Sophie delivered that last without the faintest trace of irony, for which he had to hand it to her, but it didn't seem to cheer Millie any. Clutching the lapels of her puffy blue coat with both hands, the elderly woman harrumphed at him and lumbered off like a grouchy bear that had had its supper stolen. It occurred to him that though he'd read the word plenty of times, he hadn't ever actually heard a human being harrumph before.

Once Millie was safely out of earshot, he focused his attention on Sophie, who rarely if ever had gentlemen callers, especially at midnight. And he felt an absurd urge to brush away the snowflakes that were falling gently onto her hair. Either that or wrap his arms around her and lose himself and all the pent-up anger and frustration and confusion he felt in her. He immediately squashed that jacked-up impulse—there was a reason he was here, and it wasn't to put the moves on a woman who was basically a stranger to him and possibly connected to his murdering fugitive of a father.

"One of my neighbors told me a guy about my age was hanging around outside," she said. "I thought it might be you."

"Of course you did. You're *psychic*." He wiggled his fingers at her sarcastically, pretending to shoot lightning bolts out of the tips.

"And you are poorly socialized and have awkward people skills." With that, she turned away from him and headed down the brick walkway toward Sunnyside's front gate, her heavy sandals slapping down the path, leaving tire-tread patterns in the thin layer of snow.

"I need to talk to you," he called out after her.

Without turning, she unlocked the gate and pulled it open, causing the wrought iron to creak mightily on its hinges. Just when he thought he was going to have to make a run for it and muscle his way in after her, she turned and held the gate open. He jogged toward her, needing no further invitation.

They walked into the center courtyard of the building, which was built like a giant doughnut. Apartments circled about ten stories into the air, completely surrounding the courtyard. Besides some landscaped areas that were going to need replanting soon, the interior of Sunnyside View boasted a small swimming pool, a large brick sunning area and a staff nurse who, according to the sign by the door marked with a red cross, was on call 24/7. He wondered what someone Sophie's age was doing in a place like this. He wondered what connection someone like her had to his father. He wondered why every instinct he had told him Sophie Brennan was a good person, when she obviously was hiding some sinister connection to the one human being he hated in this world. And all of that wondering made him want to shake her until she abandoned this psychic garbage and just told him the truth.

He followed her into an elevator, and she pressed the button for the eighth floor. An uncomfortable silence stretched between them as they watched the numbers slowly tick upward, until, finally, the doors opened and they both spilled gratefully into the hallway. As soon as they were inside her apartment, he sprung.

"Jack Runningwater."

"Excuse me?" A small, confused line appeared in between her eyebrows as she made her way toward the cheerful yellow kitchen that sat in the far corner of the apartment.

"Jack Runningwater. I'm playing word association with you—that's your game, isn't it?" He followed close behind, watching as she fished two glasses out of one of the cupboards. "What does that name mean to you?"

She was silent for a moment as she filled both glasses with ice water from the beat-up refrigerator's dispenser; then, she shook her head. "Absolutely nothing," she tossed out casually. Too casually, in his opinion.

He paced to the far side of her kitchen and gripped the counter with both hands. Pushing off it, he turned to stalk toward her. "Sophie, it's late, and I'm not in the mood for games," he said quietly as he closed the space between them. Anger wasn't an emotion he entertained very often, so he tried one last time to rein it in, to keep the discussion civilized, even when everything he'd been through years before suddenly felt raw and immediate. "Just tell me what you know."

Picking at the soft V neckline of her pale green sweater, she stared at the floor, her eyes unfocusing slightly as she considered his words. She appeared to concentrate for a few seconds, and then she looked up. "I don't know anything. I'm sorry, is it supposed to mean something to me?" Her words were soft and polite, too proper for his taste, too gentle for what he was feeling.

"Yes, princess, it's supposed to mean something. You know that as well as I do." He knew he was coming on too strong, knew he was probably frightening her, but the confused and angry fog that had enveloped him since Sabrina and Aaron had visited him earlier that evening had wrapped around him once more, and now he was going up and down this emotional roller coaster on autopilot.

She pushed one of the water glasses she'd filled across the counter toward him. "Alex," she said calmly. "Why don't you sit down, and drink some water, and you can tell me what you know. Then maybe I can hel—"

Lunging forward, he slammed his palm against the counter beside her, causing her to shrink abruptly away from him. "I'm not asking you to do your pretend psychic thing. You know something," he hissed. "You know him." It had been so long since he'd thought about his father—he hadn't expected it to hurt anymore. But it did, and the more he spoke to her, the more that anger bubbled up to the surface, causing him to lash out at her.

Her deep blue eyes were no longer sleepy—in fact, they looked almost afraid. Of him.

Ah, crap. It wasn't like him to try to intimidate anyone, much less a woman who was so much smaller than he was. And if he hadn't been so desperate for the truth, he might have tried the more effective and less jerk-like method of charming the information out of her first, before attempting the caveman approach. His anger lifted as suddenly as it had come, and he straightened, fully intending to back away and apologize.

That was before she pulled out the barbecue fork.

He didn't know where she'd gotten it from, but before he'd even registered that she was moving, she'd braced one hand against his chest, and the other held a large, two-pronged fork mere millimeters from his left eyeball.

"Uh, Sophie…"

"That's Princess Sophie to you." Her hand was as steady as an oak tree, and she didn't look even remotely scared of him anymore. Though her voice hadn't risen in volume, she looked like a woman who'd put a fork through his eye if she had to. "And for your information, I don't know a Jack Runningwater. I have never met a Jack Runningwater. I have no idea why you keep throwing that name in my face, though I really wish I did, because I'm a naturally curious kind of person."

Still holding the fork in place, she took her hand off his chest, glaring at it briefly as if it had touched him without her permission. "But what I do know," she continued, "is exactly what I told you before—that the murder victim you found is connected to you somehow, you're in danger and I have this nagging feeling that I should stay close to you, because I think I can keep you safe. The problem is, I want to stay close to you about as much as I want to stick this thing in my own eye." She waved the barbecue fork at him, then tossed it on the counter with a clatter, a look of mild disgust twisting her pretty mouth. "Now, I think you were just leaving."

He nodded, backing away so she'd see he wasn't a threat. "I'm sorry." He felt small and really stupid after that speech. Belatedly taking his baseball cap off his head, he ran his hands through his short hair. He didn't know why, but he suddenly wanted her to know he meant that apology. "You know, I almost believe you're not lying to me," he said. It was the closest he could come to admitting that she might not be the monster he'd created in his head.

She looked him straight in the eye. "I'm not lying to you, Alex."

He took a deep breath. If he wanted the truth, he needed to speak it himself. "But I don't believe you're psychic."

"Then believe this." She moved near enough that he could count the freckles dusting her nose, smell the scent of flowers coming from her hair. She might not be psychic, but somehow, in some definitely-not-his-type kind of way, she was magic. And he so didn't want her, of all people, to be magic. "I am not a danger to you," she continued. "I have no ill will toward you, and I would do anything, *anything* I could to prevent something bad from happening to you."

Then she reached out and closed her hand around his arm. He opened his mouth, but no words would come out.

And she gasped.

Without stopping to think about the advisability of his actions, he let his gaze drop to her lush pink mouth, knowing exactly what she'd felt the minute she'd touched him. "What, Sophie?" he murmured.

"I don't know what it is about you—" She stopped, licked her lips.

That was funny, because he didn't know what it

was about her, either. He moved closer, breathing her in, mesmerized.

"—that makes me suddenly compelled to say some really bizarre things…." She shook her head, backed away, and whatever it was that had flared up just then dissipated as the space between them grew. Her expression flattened, and she was clearly back to business; the only hint of what had just happened was the faint blush left behind on her cheeks.

"Never mind—I'm going to leave that alone for a little bit." Her eyes grew slightly unfocused as she reached up and rubbed her temple. "Humor me for a minute. Who is Jack Runningwater?"

The name was like a blast of cold water in the face. He had to get out of here. She was beautiful, and she wasn't his usual dim-and-too-skinny type, and she probably had a voodoo doll of him somewhere in her apartment that she'd bewitched. He was angry at her. He didn't trust her. He did not, could not, be even the slightest bit attracted to her. For God's sake, she *knew* something.

"Tell me," she urged.

He didn't want to, feeling the old shame he always experienced whenever anyone drew a connection between him and Jack Runningwater, but he knew he should, given that he'd been firing the name at her like a rain of bullets earlier in the conversation. At the very least, maybe revealing some of his cards would get her to inadvertently show some of hers. "Do you remember when Wilma Red Cloud was killed?"

She nodded, the line between her eyes returning as she obviously struggled to recall the details that had been splashed across newspapers and on the evening news so many years ago. "The first female tribal president of the Oglala Lakota. We read about her in school. Wasn't she murdered—"

He nodded, cutting her off. "Strangled by a man from her own tribe. No one knows why, though they suspect he was jealous, or angry that a woman was in such a powerful position." He crossed his arms over his chest and stared at the scuffed linoleum on her floor. "I have it on good authority he was just a no-good drunk."

Her expression cleared as she made the connection. "Jack Runningwater. That's the man who killed her."

"I was six," he said, not acknowledging her revelation. "I don't remember much about him. I just know one minute I had a home and a family, and the next, my mother was dragging me off the reservation and halfway across the country."

Sophie tilted her head, considering his words. "You know Wilma Red Cloud's murderer?"

He laughed, but there was no mirth behind it. "Wilma Red Cloud's murderer was my father."

"Ohhh." Her hand flew up to twist into her hair. Bringing up good old dad had always been the fastest way to kill a perfectly good conversation.

"And the police have found evidence that my father may be connected to that body I found in the woods." He arched an eyebrow at her. "As are you."

She sucked in a breath, steepling her hands in front of her mouth. "And you think that means I'm connected to your father."

"Elementary, my dear Watson."

"I'm not, Alex." She dropped her hands and moved to stand directly in front of him. "I'm just a grad student, and you said your father was a drunk. What in the world would I have to gain by collaborating with him?"

Honestly, he had no answer for that one. "You know what? This is useless." He spun around and headed for the door, suddenly feeling as if he had to get out of there or he'd suffocate. And he'd had enough of spewing out his life story to a total stranger. "I've gotta go."

"Alex, wait."

He'd managed to undo the locks and pull the door open before she closed the distance between them. And against his better judgment, he waited.

"I don't know what this means, but when I touched you a few minutes ago—" He heard her take a deep breath and exhale slowly. "The next time you see your mother…when she starts talking about yellow birds, get her out of the way." He turned to look at her, and she winced as if the words had been painful to say. "That sounds really weird, doesn't it?"

He started to reply, then just shook his head and walked away. Like he should have done a long time ago.

ROBERT FELDEN KNEW WHAT IT WAS like to be invisible. He walked the halls of the corporation every day in his not-too-expensive suits, his skin blending chameleon-like with the gray interior of the building, and his coworkers barely looked at him. He could sift into a cluster of people, and no one would even blink at his presence or acknowledge when he sifted back out again. Most of the time, he spent in his centrally located cubicle, listening quietly to the conversations around him, feeling the fabric-encased half walls closing in around him.

Day after day after day.

On the surface, it was a dreary job, a thankless job, a dead-end job with nowhere else to go but down and out. But the pay was better than anything else he could have hoped to earn as the fresh-faced, adventure-seeking army soldier he'd been, a long time ago. And that pay was more important than anything to him right now.

He stopped in the middle of the hallway and tugged his wallet out of his pocket, flipping to the plastic sleeves that contained his precious photos.

And there was his little girl, Amy, her gap-toothed seven-year-old grin bringing an answering smile to his face. She'd been in a car accident two years before, and now she could no longer run or dance with him in the kitchen the way she used to when she was younger. He'd trimmed the photo as best as he could, but he hadn't been able to eliminate every trace of metal, chrome and vinyl from the picture. It was clear exactly where Amy sat, where she would always sit.

His wife had been driving. She was gone now, and Amy was all he had.

And so he did what he had to do. To earn a good salary. To make sure that Amy had everything she needed. To try to make up for the fact that one careless moment had robbed her of the use of her legs.

He stumbled forward as one of his coworkers jostled him as she walked past. "Sorry," she murmured, barely looking up from the sheaf of papers she'd been flipping through. She didn't even see him—just knew she'd bumped into something.

They didn't know who he was. They didn't know what he could do.

He put the photo back in its sleeve and returned the wallet to the inside breast pocket of his suit jacket. His boss wanted to see him, and he knew the man didn't like to be kept waiting.

His coworkers would probably be surprised if they knew the real reason he'd been hired by the corporation. But it was part of his job to keep that knowledge a secret, to be in the office but not really part of it, to stay on the fringes. To be invisible.

He slipped into the stairwell and climbed the

five flights to the penthouse office at the top of the building. Using a key for which there were only two other copies, he slipped into the penthouse lobby, pushed through the double doors to the main area and moved silently past the receptionist's empty desk—she was on her brief lunch break. And then he was inside.

The CEO's space was opulent, with floors made of some exotic wood—carefully cut and laid so no knotholes showed through the gleaming finish. The furniture was upholstered in a dark butter-soft leather, and the ornate tables scattered about probably cost more than his yearly salary, considerable as it was.

He approached the CEO's desk, and without preamble, the great man spun around in his high-backed office chair to face Robert.

"Some information of a sensitive nature has been leaked, Robert."

He nodded, waiting for the man to go on.

The CEO folded his hands over his sizable paunch, encased in an expensive shirt made of fine linen, hand-tailored so the buttons wouldn't strain no matter which way the big man moved. "We've taken care of the leak…"

Robert knew exactly how the leak had been "taken care of."

"…and now we need to take care of the person who is now in possession of sensitive information."

His boss had grown soft-looking through the

years, while Robert himself had only grown harder, leaner. But the CEO could do that—he had Robert to be his eyes and ears, to be his left hand, the one that operated in secret.

Robert cleared his throat, not trusting his voice to work properly, he'd been silent for so long today. "He's gone underground again, I assume?" he asked. "We've been looking for him for twenty years. With all due respect, sir, what makes you think we'll find him now?"

The CEO sat up, the well-oiled hinges of his chair barely making a sound. "I don't want you to find him." He pivoted to look out the expanse of windows behind him at the cold, gray waters of Puget Sound. "Runningwater," he murmured. "Who knew that after all this time, that mosquito would become a bigger threat than we could imagine?"

A slow thrill pooled in the bottom of Robert's stomach at his boss's words, as he waited for the man to issue orders. Once again. Finally. He'd been penned up inside that cubicle for so long, growing pale in the perpetual Seattle dampness, and maybe even growing a little softer himself. But now, once again, finally, he'd be able to perform the skills for which he'd been hired, do the things he was born to do.

"I don't want you to find him," the CEO repeated. "I want you to go after his family."

His coworkers had no idea that the thin, balding, nondescript man in cubicle forty-seven could break adult bones with his bare hands, could shoot a gun from across five football fields and still hit his target, could kill a man twice his size without feeling even the remotest twinge of guilt.

He thought of the picture in his wallet. "That won't be a problem, sir."

You did what you had to do. Good thing he also enjoyed it.

Chapter Five

Whenever Alex asked Anna Gray about the father he could barely remember, her response usually ran something along the lines of "Don't trouble yourself about him. You have me now." And the implication that Anna should be enough for him had always shut him up—because she'd worked until her hands were dry and cracked to make sure he had not just food and a roof over his head, but nice clothes and the latest toys. She'd let her own hobbies and dates with her friends fall by the wayside so she could cheer him on when he'd played basketball—fifth bleacher, center court, every game. After putting herself through night school and getting a job as Port Renegade Elementary School's librarian, she'd also kept her old job cleaning classrooms at the local university, to make sure he could attend on a reduced rate as a staff member's son. She had been more than enough for him. But he still wondered about his father. He'd just always kept that to himself.

But now, that had to change, given that good old Dad was traipsing about town with a garrote and some sort of insane plan that Alex couldn't even begin to comprehend. As he pulled into the circular driveway in front of Anna's two-story 1920s home, flanked on each side by a stand of evergreens, he knew the time had come for him to press his mother for more details about her ex-husband. The thought sat on his chest like a too-heavy set of dumbbells, and his mind couldn't help but replay the way the natural sparkle in her eyes had always disappeared whenever the word *father* passed his lips. But the crow carrier's message couldn't be ignored. Jack Runningwater was here, in Port Renegade, and she deserved to know that. And Alex himself needed to know if that meant his only living family member was in any kind of danger.

Anna's front door swung open before he'd even cleared the front steps.

"Alex!" With a quickness that hinted at the natural athlete she was—she'd taught him to play basketball and had out-hiked him until he was well into his teens—Anna Gray bolted across her porch to wrap him in her sturdy embrace. He put his arms around her small frame, careful not to catch her long black braid with his all-weather sports watch.

"I was going to call you." She pulled back, patting his arm and revealing the familiar chipped canine with her wide smile. "I made fudge."

Native American mothers from tribal nations

across the country often fattened up their children with fry bread. Anna, who'd left the Oglala behind years ago, made fudge—a bewildering range of varieties of fudge. He followed her into the kitchen and grabbed a piece from the nearest pan, which had a peanut butter layer on top. Smooth, creamy and not too sweet, it melted in his mouth and made him automatically reach for another.

"What's the occasion?" he asked, shucking his coat and pulling up a chair beside her dining-room table, on which lay no less than four pans of fudge. The one nearest him had cherries mixed in, and he cut himself a sample of that as well, using a chocolate-encrusted knife she'd left on the table. It was a good thing he didn't still live at home or he'd be so overweight from all the candy, he'd be one of those people who had to call the fire department to chisel him out of the bathtub after he got stuck.

"We're having a bake sale to raise funds for the library." She reached behind her back to untie her yellow flowered apron and tugged it off, draping it over the back of one of her dining-table chairs. After relocating a few pans from the table to her kitchen counters, she sat down across from him.

"So, what's up?"

He scratched both hands through his hair, not having expected her to get to the point so quickly, and realizing that he should have known she would. She had that mother's sixth sense whenever something was troubling him.

"Well…uh…nothing?" As soon as he said it, he wanted to kick himself for being so lame…not to mention transparent.

She folded her arms across the tabletop, the deep red color of her fitted top bringing out a rosy color in her cheeks. "Alex, I'm your mother. After twenty-six years of this, I'd think you would stop trying to fool me." She smiled gently and waited.

Shoving a piece of rocky-road fudge into his mouth, he pointed at his face as he chewed, silently conveying that he couldn't talk to her with his mouth full. She simply watched him, her placid expression never changing. It always had been pretty much inevitable that whenever he wanted to keep something from her, Anna would eventually wear him down and he'd end up telling her everything. He just wished he didn't have to tell her this.

After he'd chewed, swallowed, faked chewing and swallowed again, Alex figured he'd stalled long enough. "Mom, I need to know about my father."

Her eyes grew so wide, he could see a line of white around the dark brown irises. She started to push back from the table, but he leaned forward and placed his hand over one of hers, stopping her.

"I know you don't want to talk about him, and I've tried not push you, but…" He paused, wondering how he could find the words to make her not want to clam up and bolt, as she always had. On instinct, he went for the shocking truth with no preliminaries to soften the blow. "Mom, I think he's in Washington. I think he may have killed someone."

At her sharp inhalation, he looked up, only to find that his mother—who had always been stunning, so much so that he'd had to biff a few of his friends in the head after they'd commented in not-so-politically-correct ways on her looks—suddenly appeared frail and small and every one of her fifty-three years. The skin on her fine-boned face sagged, her shoulders slumped, and her full mouth turned downward in a frown that added years to her. It was probably one of the most painful moments of his life, and he hated that he'd have to keep pushing until he learned the truth, once and for all.

Still holding her hand, the only part of her that usually hinted at her true age, he told her about the body he'd found, about Aaron's assertion that the ritual aspect was most likely a copycat cover-up, and about the crow feather. At the mention of the last, she shook her head, again and again, as if the movement would make the thing untrue. And still, she didn't say a word.

"Are you in danger?" He ducked his head to try to get into her line of sight. But she wouldn't look at him, instead choosing to keep her focus on their hands or the tabletop.

"No," she said finally. "No, we're not in danger."

"Mom, it's time to tell me," he said gently. "I've tried to respect that you didn't want to talk about…

him. I wouldn't ask unless I had no choice." When she didn't respond, he tried again, hoping to shake her out of her silence with the sheer force of his words. "There's a body in the morgue tonight, and save for a few creative details, the method of killing was the same as when he murdered Wilma Red Cloud. The calling card he left behind is the same."

She shook her head again, her breathing growing rapid and hitched.

"Why did Runningwater kill Wilma Red Cloud? Why would he kill someone here, now, after all these years?" She still didn't answer, but instead of feeling impatient, he just felt tenderness, and a deep sadness he couldn't name. He pushed away from the table and walked around to crouch at her feet and grip her arms, trying to tell her through touch how important this was. "Will he come here? Does he want to hurt you?" He blew out a harsh breath, nearly overcome at the thought of losing his mother in the way that someone else had lost that man he'd found in the woods. "Tell me, Mom. Please."

Something in his voice finally brought her out of her shock, and she reached up to brush her fingertips along his hairline. "Your father didn't kill Wilma Red Cloud, Alex."

It took him a few minutes to process that sentence. "He— What?" The thought was ridiculous, something she was just throwing out there to keep him from worrying about her. Of course Jack Runningwater had killed Wilma Red Cloud. For the love of God, Alex had learned about the murder in elementary school, during Women's History Month, when one of his teachers had read mini-biographies of notable modern women daily for the entire damned month of March, and the first female leader of the Oglala Lakota had been mini-bio number seven. He'd lived his whole life carrying the knowledge that his father was a drunk and had murdered a national freaking role model for the ages, and his mother had never, ever bothered to tell him otherwise.

Then again, had she ever actually acknowledged that the story was true?

He sat back on his haunches and scrubbed a hand down his face. He'd always just assumed they'd moved off the reservation out of shame. And Anna had always told him that he had no reason to be afraid. *Don't worry about that, Alex. You have me now.*

"Jack didn't kill her. He just took the fall for it."

He couldn't believe what he was hearing. "And it took you twenty-six years to tell me that my father isn't the crazed fugitive killer I've grown up thinking he was?" He sprang to his feet, his voice growing louder with each word. "What the hell, Mom? You think I might have not liked to know that my family history doesn't include murderous wack-job genes?"

"Alex—"

"Don't 'Alex' me. You lied to me."

Her spine went ramrod straight. "I never lied to you." She tilted her head then, as if reconsidering that obviously erroneous position. "Okay, I concealed some things from you, but—"

"Some things?" He threw his hands into the air. "How about one really big thing?"

"Sweetheart, you've been my whole life ever since your father disappeared. Everything we ever did was for you." She rose and padded over to him, her entire expression one of pleading. For him to comprehend something incomprehensible.

"I want the truth, Mom. I'm not a child anymore, and I want every last detail."

She exhaled slowly, her shoulders slumping once more, and she nodded. "You're right. It's time. But I have to go." She swept an arm out to indicate the pans of fudge lining her kitchen counters. "I have a bake sale to run. The kids are counting on me to have enough money in my budget to keep them in *Princess Diaries* and Harry Potter books until they go off to the middle school." She twisted her hands together, and he noticed that she was having a hard time meeting his eyes. "Come for dinner, and I'll tell you everything you want to know tonight."

There wasn't much more to say after that, so the two of them started working in silence, covering the pans in plastic wrap and transporting them out to her car. Once he'd gathered up the last pan, he stepped outside and waited for her to lock her front door. As she twisted the key in the lock, she started to speak.

"Just remember, your father isn't a saint," she said to the door. "And even if he wasn't a killer years ago, that doesn't mean years of being on the run haven't turned him into one." She turned toward him then, the sadness on her face causing him to flash back to the day they'd left the reservation when he was six. "Whatever happens, you need to promise me you'll stay out of this. This is bigger than our little family, bigger than you can imagine."

They hadn't been a whole family since he could remember, but although he was strongly tempted to point that out, he swallowed the sentence. Even if he couldn't think of a good reason for anyone to lie to her son about his roots, his whole history, maybe there was a chance that she'd had one. Knowing his mother, he knew that no matter how misguided her actions may have been, she undoubtedly had had his best interests in mind. "I can't promise that, Mom."

"You'll have to, or you won't hear one more thing from me, sonny boy." She pulled back and poked him with one finger just beneath his collar-bone. He had to smile at her attempt to inject some levity into the heaviest conversation of his life. And then her expression grew serious once more. "Forgive me, Alex. I just wanted to protect— Oh."

"What?" He turned to follow her line of sight. A light brown older Ford of some kind was driving leisurely down the street.

"Just a moment of déjà vu." She put her hand to

her forehead to block out the setting sun and watched the Ford move toward them. "An old friend of mine used to drive a car like that."

"Ah." He started heading back to her car, so he could put her candy in it and get her on her way.

"Connie Yellow Bird. I haven't thought about her in age—"

That name… It nagged at him, like a long-forgotten childhood event that someone else had brought up. "Who's that, Mom?"

The car slowed as it neared Anna's house.

"Connie Yellow Bird? Just an old fr—"

The whole world faded away, bringing the creeping car into sharp focus. A few of his scattered memories finally connected and they hit him like a bucket of ice in the face.

The passenger-side window started to roll down.

With a sharp curse, he whirled around, ignoring his mother's yelp of consternation when he dropped the pan he'd been holding. "Mom, go back inside!"

"What's wrong?" Instead of turning around, she started moving toward him, one arm outstretched. "You look—"

He ran for her, as fast and as hard as he could, fully intending to tackle her to the ground if he had to. A sharp crack filled the air, so loud it was almost painful.

But everything happened too fast and all he could do was watch as his mother fell, her head hitting the ground, hard.

In the next instant he was kneeling beside her,

touching her to reassure himself she was still alive. It was then he realized that his hands were covered with something warm, sticky. He couldn't bear to look at them, to discover what it was.

"Oh, no. Mom, come on. Oh, God, no. Mom." His voice cracked on the words, but somehow, in spite of the horror he felt, his training took over and he remembered to check for a pulse, to cover the hole in her chest with his hand and not let go, to watch his mother's blood pump through his fingers without crumbling into a useless heap beside her. He fumbled for his cell phone and automatically dialed 911, not allowing himself to entertain the possibility of losing his only living family member.

When she starts talking about yellow birds, get her out of the way.

But he hadn't really listened until it was too late. And that could cost him everything.

As Sophie approached her front door, she slipped her arm out of the carrying strap of her brown canvas-and-leather tote, letting it fall to the ground to give her aching shoulder a break. The cheap bag was filled to almost bursting with books she planned to use for her mini term paper on the theme of alienation in three works by Degas, Hopper and Segal, and lugging it all the way from her Saturday library study session had felt like carrying a small car on her back. She slipped her key into the lock just in time to hear the phone start ringing inside her apartment.

Of course. That stupid phone didn't ring half as often as she'd like, and when it did, it always seemed to perversely do so when she would be forced to scramble for it. Then again, it was probably her mother. She'd called her back after returning from the police station, reassuring her that everything was all right. But of course, her mom had taken the opportunity to lecture her about ignoring her "intuitive impulses" and stop sticking her nose in where it didn't belong.

Shoving the door open, she kicked her bag inside and made a beeline for the phone, managing to pick it up before the answering machine kicked in.

"Sophie?"

Oh, God. Her heart 'actually tripped a bit at the sound of Alex's baritone coming through the line. She told herself it was because she half expected him to start hurling accusations at her again. "Um, yeah. Hi." Cradling the phone between her cheek and a hunched-up shoulder, she shrugged out of her coat, more than a little curious about what he wanted.

"Hey, I—" She heard him exhale in a whoosh of air. "Look, I don't know how to ask you this, but—" His voice was softer than it had usually been when he'd spoke to her, and he'd never talked in fits and starts like this. She bent down to unzip her boots.

"I'm at the hospital," he finally blurted. "Can you come?"

Her pulse skipped at the word *hospital*, and she

straightened, deciding that maybe her boots ought to stay on. "Are you okay?"

"I'm fine." Another pause. "I know I don't have the right to ask you for any favor—"

"I'm on my way," she interrupted. As much as it usually annoyed her inner feminist to jump just because a hot guy asked her to, there was something…lost in the sound of his voice, something that made her want to see what she could do to help. "Just tell me what room you're in."

She got the directions from him and in less than fifteen minutes was walking toward the hospital's glass double doors, which swished open as she approached. Port Renegade General was a small, easily navigable hospital, so she headed for the elevator without pausing at the information desk. A quick glance at the floor plan that took up nearly the entire front lobby wall told her room 517, the one Alex had asked her to come to, was in the intensive care unit. She couldn't even imagine who he'd come to see.

When she reached the fifth floor, the doors opened to reveal a tired-looking nurse behind a U-shaped counter, scrawling something in a binder.

"May I help you?" she asked, not looking up from her work.

"Uh, I'm here to see…" Who *was* Sophie here to see? All she had was a room number. "The Grays," she guessed. "Alex Gray called me. Room 517."

"Go down the hall to your right, it's the fifth

door on your left past the bathrooms." The nurse waved her pen in the direction of room 517 and then returned her attention to the mountain of paperwork in front of her.

"Thanks." Sophie walked quickly down the hall, trying not to look into the rooms as she sped past them, her boots squeaking on the pristine white-speckled tile. All of those people with tubes coming out of them, surrounded by machines and desperate loved ones made her ache. That was why she had never been cut out to study medicine—besides the fact that she had hated biology and had gotten her one and only high school C in the class for refusing to dissect a frog on moral grounds—she got too caught up in people's personal stories and wouldn't be able to detach enough to figure out what was wrong with them and how to fix it.

When she reached room 517, she paused at the doorway, bracing herself before looking inside. A dark-haired woman lay unconscious on the bed, a breathing tube lodged in her throat and monitors flashing various readings around her. Alex sat by her bed in jeans and a gray hooded sweatshirt, sans baseball cap. He must have been there for a while because he'd laid his head on the edge of the mattress and had fallen asleep in what looked like a really uncomfortable position, still holding the woman's limp hand.

The sign by the door read Anna Gray. Probably

his mother, though she looked almost young enough to be his sister, even with the trach tube and hospital gown. It must be awful to see someone he loved in such a vulnerable state.

Sophie stepped inside the room and touched him lightly on the shoulder. "Alex, I'm here," she whispered, figuring if that quiet announcement didn't rouse him, she'd make herself comfortable in the room's other chair and wait until he woke naturally.

But he sat up as soon as she said his name. "Soph?"

His deep brown eyes usually had a sharp, almost predatory look to them, the in-your-face intensity that was helped along by a slightly aquiline nose and the dark slashes of his eyebrows. But now, as he came out of an undoubtedly fitful sleep, they were almost soft, vulnerable. His full mouth parted slightly, and heaven help her, he looked almost glad to see her.

"Hi." She sat then, and after blinking the sleep out of his eyes, he scooted his chair around to face her. "Your mom?" she asked gently.

He nodded, scrubbing a hand through his dark, glossy hair, which was so short, it looked exactly the same when he was through.

"What happened?"

He told her about the brown car and the gunshot that had resulted in a bullet lodging itself in her chest, collapsing her lung. Anna Gray had hit her head hard when she'd fallen after being shot, so she also had a mild concussion, but nothing that would have resulted in doctors having to induce a coma.

"They had to perform emergency surgery, and she reacted badly to the anesthesia, and, uh…" She knew he was trying to recall whatever explanation the medical personnel had given him, and his brown eyes had more than a trace of sadness in them, mingling with the exhaustion of sitting in a hospital all day. "She ended up breathing in her own vomit. Apparently, she has something called aspiration pneumonia now, and they had to knock her out for a while to put that in her." He gestured with one hand at the trach tube, connected to a machine that hissed regularly behind her bed, breathing for her. "That must hurt like hell," he said softly.

In the middle of all the IVs and monitors attached to Mrs. Gray, Sophie spotted another tube snaking out from under the covers on her left side, probably for the collapsed lung. Alex was right— if she hadn't been anesthetized, she'd probably be in a tremendous amount of pain. "I'm so sorry." It still didn't answer the question of why he'd called her here, instead of the many friends he must have in the area, growing up here as he had. But she wasn't about to rush him into an explanation.

He rested his elbows on the mattress, taking his mother's hand once more in both of his. "Can she hear me? When I talk to her?"

Well, that was unexpected. She narrowed her

eyes at him, trying to assess the motivation behind his words. It was an odd question, and what was even stranger was that he asked it as if he completely trusted whatever answer she gave him. She would have loved to have been able to read Anna Gray's mind right then, but as was usually the case when she was under the least amount of pressure, she drew a big fat blank. So she told him the truth.

"I don't know. I'd like to think so."

His mouth flattened, and then he nodded. "You're probably wondering why I asked you to come here."

Without thinking about what she was doing, she reached out and traced a finger lightly along his hairline. "It doesn't matter. You shouldn't be alone right now." Realizing what she was doing, she pulled her hand back, feeling a furious blush rising up her neck to undoubtedly turn her fair complexion tomato-red.

He laughed softly, and all Sophie could think was that he couldn't possibly be looking at her the way he was looking at her. She busied her hands with unbuttoning her coat, so she wouldn't have to look at him. "How long will she have to be like this?"

"I don't know." Alex threw his hands up, then let them drop to his sides. "They won't give me a time frame. I asked them whether she was going to be all right, and they wouldn't say anything about that, either, other than that her condition is serious—

thank you, Dr. Obvious." He sat back in his chair, chewing the inside of his cheek as he watched the blank wall across the room. "Reading between the lines, I'd say that's not good."

Slipping her coat off, she let it crumple into the chair. "Do you have any idea who did this to her?"

"Other than my father? Not a clue. Mom said he wouldn't hurt her." His face darkened—he obviously didn't share his mother's optimism on that topic. With a sigh, he stood abruptly and walked to the sole window in the room, leaning against the wall beside it and looking outside. Through the glass, still speckled with moisture from where the afternoon snow had hit it, she could see the twinkling lights of downtown. He grew almost transfixed by them, and she merely watched him and waited until he felt like talking again.

For a time, the only sound in the room was the beeping of Anna's monitors, the whoosh of air in and out of her breathing tube. Then, Alex raised a fist to his mouth and yawned, stretching his elbows up and out in a way that caused his lightweight sweatshirt to ride up and expose a stretch of tanned, flat stomach, muscles that she could actually see bunching and pulling with his movement. And unexpectedly, she was hit by a wave of desire so strong, she had to clench the armrests of her chair to keep herself from getting up and putting her hands on that smooth skin, up and under his shirt, until she had had her fill of touching him.

Breathe, Sophie. You'd think she'd never seen a man's bare chest before, much less a few harmless inches of skin. She really had to get her head out of her books and go out on a date soon, or she'd throw herself at that too-gorgeous man, and he'd…

He'd laugh at her. Guys who looked like that didn't look at women like her. Average women.

She could practically hear her mother now. "He's out of your league, honey. Why don't you try someone else?"

You'd probably scare him anyway.

She rubbed her suddenly moist palms on her jeans, glad that his attention was still on the streets below and not on her. It was so inappropriate to think about him like this, too, what with his poor, sick mother lying only a few feet away. She didn't even know where those thoughts had come from— stupid, useless, unfounded, out-of-nowhere crush. She barely knew him.

"I don't understand—"

His voice broke into her thoughts, and she looked up guiltily, her face flushing once more— the curse of the fair-skinned redhead. But thankfully, he didn't seem to notice her discomfort, nor could he apparently read minds, since he wasn't running down the hallway screaming.

He pushed off the wall and approached her, half sitting, half leaning on his mother's bed, so he was mere inches from where she sat. "My mother mentioned her friend Connie Yellow Bird, and then…"

He turned his face abruptly away, but she could tell by the tension in his lean frame that he was close to losing control. "Someone shot her. And I didn't get to her fast enough."

She dug her nails into her hands to keep from touching him, even if just to offer comfort. "You couldn't have."

"Maybe." They stayed like for a moment, him standing, and her sitting so close. She knew he was struggling with what had happened, with the prediction she'd made. Finally, he continued, craning his head to look down at his mother instead of at her.

"In my head, I know what you claim to be isn't possible. But in here—" he thumped a fist lightly against his heart "—I feel like you're the only connection to my father I have left. There's so much she didn't tell me." He turned again and locked his eyes on hers. "And either you're one hell of a liar, or you're the only person I can count on to tell me the truth."

So he still didn't believe her, not entirely. And short of giving him a blow-by-blow prediction of every event that would take place in the next half hour—which was so beyond her capabilities, especially under pressure—she had no clue how to make him understand that she wasn't out to hurt him. To tell the truth, she'd really had it with trying. "So, basically you called me down here to imply that I'm a freak, and ask for my help?"

Gathering her purse off the floor, she stood and slid her arm through the strap so it rested on her shoulder. As she made her way to the door, she trailed her fingers along the edge of Anna's bed, brushing the woman's hand lightly with her own. A thought flitted through Sophie's mind. She pushed it aside. "I'm not a liar. But I think you'll have to decide that for yourself."

Just then, the same nurse who'd been at the front desk popped her head into the room, her blond hair falling out of the clip she'd tried using to hold it out of her face. "Mr. Gray? I'm sorry, but visiting hours are over in five minutes." She bit her lip, looking genuinely apologetic. "Your friend will have to go, unless she's family."

"She was just leaving," he replied, an empty, un-readable expression on his face. Apparently, he didn't much care about having implied she was a freak. Probably because it was the truth.

"Right." Sophie hitched her shoulder, so the nurse could see from her purse's position that she had already prepared to depart. The woman nodded kindly and left.

She headed for the door, pausing with her hand on the doorjamb at the last minute, the thought she'd had a few seconds earlier growing stronger and more insistent. "She can hear you," she blurted out, driven by an impulse so strong she could barely control it. Alex had already resumed his place at his mother's side, but her words made him look up, his expression one of clear surprise. "And she's worried about you, Crow Carrier."

With that, Sophie left the room, scurrying down the hall before he could make her feel any worse about herself. Crow Carrier? Where the heck had that come from?

Oh, God, what if that meant absolutely nothing to him, and he thought she was making fun of his Native American heritage? She jabbed several times at the down button for the elevator, praying that it would come quickly so she could escape. Ugh, she might as well have started dancing around the room doing some kind of caricatured war whoop and really gone all out to offend him.

Finally, the elevator doors opened and she stepped gratefully inside. Blessedly, no one wanted to get on the thing and she was able to zip all the way down to the ground floor, and in seconds, she was in the parking lot and closing in on her battered Mazda 3. Weaving her way through the remaining vehicles between her and escape, she noticed that someone had stuck a small slip of paper under her windshield-wiper blade that she really, really hoped wasn't a ticket. "Please don't let me have parked in a fire lane," she mumbled, fishing in her purse for the keys.

Using her electronic key fob to unlock the car with one hand, she tugged on the paper with the other until it came free. It wasn't a ticket, and unless local businesses were getting lazy about designing their flyers, it wasn't an advertisement either.

She scanned the note once, and because it confused her, she read it again, more slowly. The menace behind the words finally sank in the second time.

Dear Miss Brennan,
Alex Gray is a dangerous person to be around. For your own safety, put your head back in your books.
Your friend

Chapter Six

The first time Sophie heard the floorboard squeak, she rolled over, still mostly asleep, tugging her quilts and comforter around her shoulder and figuring she'd dreamed it. The second time, a little more awake now, she still dismissed it as the normal sounds of the building settling.

The third time, she knew someone was in her apartment.

On the other side of her half-closed bedroom door, someone coughed softly—a barely there sound that under normal circumstances she wouldn't have noticed at all. But now, with her senses on high alert, it sent adrenaline shooting through her body, driving away sleep and causing every one of her muscles to contract to the point where it was almost painful. Her first impulse was to throw off the covers and bolt for the front door— the one and only exit that wasn't an eighth-story window—but she took a deep, shaky breath and forced herself to remain still. Her apartment's open design made running out impossible—no matter where the intruder was, with the exceptions of the laundry closet and bathroom, he'd be able to see her. And, most likely, intercept her.

Keenly aware of the noise of her own breathing and her heartbeat, she strained to see in the pitch dark of her bedroom. The shadows of her dresser, the thin slice of moonlight peeking out from the side of her room-darkening shades and the dark maw of her open closet were all easily discernible, but it was the faint outline of her almost-closed bedroom door that she focused all of her attention on.

Someone was behind that door.

The soft whisper of fabric brushing fabric told her that he was most likely in the living-room area and was navigating around her couch. Then came the faint crackle of papers being quietly shuffled— all the books and stacks of mail she'd left on her coffee table, no doubt. God, he was going through her things.

Her heart started hammering so loudly, she was sure he could hear it, and it made listening for his next move nearly impossible. Knowing she couldn't continue to just lie in bed and wait for him, she slowly, carefully slid inch by painstaking inch out toward the side of the mattress, trying not to alert him to the fact that she was awake. She'd almost gotten free of the covers when the mattress springs creaked with her movement. She froze, her body half on, half off the bed.

Dead silence greeted her from the next room.

Breathe in.

Breathe out.

Wait for him to come get her.

A few endless seconds later, the paper shuffling began again. Sophie slid off the bed into a relieved heap on the carpeted floor of her bedroom, safe for now. But how long did she have, really?

Focus, Brennan. What does he want? How can you use that to your advantage? Clutching the edge of the mattress as if it were a security blanket, she crouched behind her bed, trying to calm herself and not give in to the choking panic that made it hard to breathe, much less function on a higher level.

The faint sounds from the main area of her apartment told her this was no ordinary break-in. He was definitely looking for something, rather than attempting to steal her TV and cheap portable stereo. But what could she, an impoverished grad student, have that anyone capable of slipping past the building's ad hoc security and through a locked door would want?

A mental calculation of her meager belongings quickly led her to the conclusion that the intruder could very well just be looking for money before he came for her. And what he planned to do to her, the lone twentysomething female in the entire building with no family in the area and no one around to protect her but a bunch of card-carrying AARP members, she didn't even want to consider.

Speaking of nosy Millie and the geriatric Neighborhood Watch, where on earth were they? How could a burglar or…worse have gotten past them?

What had he *done* to them?

Alex Gray.

The name came to her as if someone had whispered it in her ear, and suddenly she knew beyond a shadow of a doubt that whoever was in her home was connected in some way to Alex. And his mother. Who was lying in a hospital bed fighting for her life after being shot.

She really wished she hadn't been too cheap to buy a second phone for her bedroom, if not the cell phone her mother was always nagging her to get. Because now the only phone was in her kitchen, mere steps away from the living area where he was. She could get to the phone, but she'd never be able to dial it.

Soft footfalls on the hardwood floors outside her bedroom had her clutching the mattress even tighter. He was on the move.

A shadow fell across her bedroom floor, blocking the faint moonlight that had streamed through her partly open door. He couldn't see her yet. But all it would take was the slightest push and he'd be inside, they'd be face-to-face. Her eyes darted around the room, trying to come up with something she could use as a weapon, but she couldn't see anything that would fend off a fully grown male. No Mace, no gun, no baseball bat, nothing but her bare hands and the flimsy iron stick of a bedside lamp she'd bought at a garage sale last month.

She reached for the lamp. The shadow grew larger.

She didn't know how long they remained like that—he hovering by her door, she crouched behind her mattress with one hand clutching her lamp, trying not to move, to make a sound, trying to keep from screaming. But then he finally moved off, and though Sophie nearly collapsed with relief, she knew that his decision not to enter was probably only temporary. With quiet, restrained movements, she unplugged the lamp and carefully lifted it off the nightstand, rising to her feet as she did so. Slowly, she wrapped the cord around its base, creating a more effective, if flimsy, weapon, which she brandished in front of her like a club.

A few seconds later, she heard something that made her scalp prickle as a scream rose in her throat—the sing of metal against wood, once, twice, again. Gripping the lamp so tightly she'd cut off circulation to her fingers, she tried to quiet the panic that had her gasping for air in stifled, terrified sobs.

He was taking her knives out of the butcher block on her kitchen counter.

And he had her cornered.

ALEX DIDN'T KNOW HOW LONG he'd sat there at his mother's side. The nurses came in, checked the monitors, changed the IV bags, and the nurses went out. He just sat there through it all, holding his mother's hand and praying for a sign that she was still there, somewhere. He'd thought once that she might have squeezed his fingers in response to some inane thing he'd said, but then he'd opened his eyes and discovered that he'd only been dreaming.

"Come on, Mom," he whispered to the still figure before him. "Come on." It was the only thing he could think of to say anymore.

Sometime during the evening, one of the nurses had paused in the middle of her vital sign checks to tell him that it was a good sign that Anna's blood oxygen levels had stabilized—a small sign of progress when she had a long climb ahead of her, but he'd take even that little bit of good news over nothing at all. He'd thanked her, she'd left, and he'd spent the next two hours watching the numbers on the oxygen monitor go up a single digit, then go back down, go up two, then go back down. As if he could keep the figure stable if he just concentrated hard enough. His head felt thick and his body ponderous with exhaustion, but he couldn't go to sleep now. Not when he had to keep those damn numbers from plummeting when he wasn't looking.

The measured voice of a local newscaster came into the room from the small television mounted up near the ceiling, delivering a teaser about shots ringing out in a quiet well-to-do Port Renegade neighborhood. Knowing that the story would no doubt feature his mother and her quiet well-to-do neighborhood, Alex reached for the remote and switched the set off. As soon as he had, he noticed that his cell phone was quietly playing the opening notes to "Freebird."

He palmed it off the small bedside table and flicked it open. "Alex Gray."

"Alex, it's Aaron." Something in the detective's voice instantly alerted him that all was not well.

"What's wrong? Is Sabrina okay?" Dropping his mother's hand, he pushed himself off the mattress so he was sitting up straight.

"Yeah, Sabrina's fine, but… Have you been spending time with Sophie Brennan lately?"

Sophie? Rubbing the bridge of his nose, Alex wondered how to answer that question. And then he remembered the brown sedan that had rolled past his mother's house today, remembered catching his mother as she fell. "Is she— Did something happen?" Oh, God, not Sophie. Please don't let them have gotten to Sophie.

Through the line, he heard the detective inhale through his teeth. "Yeah. We're at her apartment right now. She's—"

"I'm sorry, Mr. Gray, but you're not allowed to use cell phones in the hospital," a chirpy blonde wearing a pink volunteer's smock interrupted.

She'd been in and out with magazines and ice water all night, generally smiling inanely at him the entire time. Alex fought the urge to shout at her to leave him the hell alone.

"Sure, just a second." He ducked his head, his hand curled protectively on the phone. "Donovan, what happened to her?" His voice sounded louder to his ears than he'd intended.

"No, Mr. Gray, now." The woman strode in and, with a quickness he wouldn't have expected from someone so tiny and cheerful, her hand darted out and snatched his phone from him. She snapped it shut, Aaron's reply lost in the mini-scuffle. "Hospital rules," she singsonged. "I know most let you make calls now, but ours…"

He could only stare at her as she handed it back to him. "You're welcome to take it into the parking lot and finish your call." With a brilliant smile and a toss of her blonde pixie cut, she bounded out of the room, her orthopedic shoes squeaking with every step.

Alex looked at his mother, hardly wanting to leave her alone, but unable to stay now that something may have happened to Sophie. Whatever her role in this whole mess was, it had put her in danger. *He'd* put her in danger.

And now, for all he knew, she might be in the same situation as his mom. Maybe worse.

Maybe she was gone.

Clamping down on the awful thought, Alex

grabbed his jacket from the chair Sophie had been sitting in hours before and performed an awkward one-handed maneuver to get himself into it.

As a precautionary measure—and probably because they'd known each other for a couple of years now—Detective Donovan had arranged for a Port Renegade police officer to stand guard in front of Anna Gray's hospital room, just in case her still-at-large assailant got any ideas about finishing what he'd started. As Alex left his mother's room, he told the cop he'd be leaving for a while, asking him to take extra care that no one went into the room other than hospital personnel. Once he'd gotten the man's assurance that no one was getting near his mom without a lab coat, a badge or a nurse's smock—especially not the candy striper they seriously needed to fire—he ran down the hallway, heading for the exit. As soon as he burst outside the hospital doors, he tried Aaron on his cell phone, but the man's line kept going to voice mail.

Unable to deal with not knowing what had happened to Sophie, Alex murmured an apology up toward his mother's window and got into his truck. It took him less than fifteen minutes to navigate the quiet streets of Port Renegade to Sophie's apartment complex, which he found surrounded by police cars, whose flashing lights bathed the building and grounds in an eerie, flickering red light. The complex gates had been propped open, so he ran through them unchallenged, heading for the elevator.

A couple of cops roaming the courtyard spotted him, but since Port Renegade wasn't the largest city in the world, he knew them, so they merely nodded at him and then let him be. He jabbed at the buttons with an impatient thumb, but when the elevator proved to be one of the world's slowest, taking its sweet time about crawling down from the fourth floor, he opted for the stairs instead.

He took them two at a time until he finally reached the eighth floor. Years of tracking in the Olympic Mountains and rock climbing in his spare time had put him in excellent shape, so he wasn't even close to winded when he burst through the fire door and into the hallway.

And relief hit him like a two-by-four to the chest when he saw Sophie standing a few feet in front of him, clutching with both hands at the lapels of her dark brown sweater, the hemline of which hit her at midthigh. He couldn't speak, couldn't even think. So he did the only thing he could do—he moved. Toward her.

The heavy steel door slammed shut behind him and she turned at the sound. He opened his mouth to say something to her, but still the words wouldn't come, as if he were choking on his own relief. She'd been crying, her flushed cheeks still shiny with dampness.

"Alex?" She took a few steps in his direction, and without stopping to think, he did the same, catching her by the arms and then—in an act that would have been against his better judgment if he'd been thinking at all—he pulled her to him. He wrapped one arm around her waist, intending to offer her comfort and nearly losing his breath at the feel of her.

"Sophie." Speech returned at last, in the form of her name. He threaded his fingers through her amazing hair, reveling in the fact that he could still touch her. "I thought something had…I thought you were…" He couldn't even finish that thought.

"You shouldn't have left your mother. I'm fine," she said, her breath warm on his neck. Her fierce grip on his shoulders belied her words.

"Damn, Sophie," he whispered, and then, still not in his right mind, he kissed her.

Her mouth was warm and soft, and tasted like salt from her tears. She froze in surprise at first, but it didn't take long before she kissed him back, still clinging to him, and he thought he'd die if he didn't get her somewhere more private than a hallway. And all he could think was how much he wanted her, of how he'd kill anyone with his bare hands who tried to get near her and hurt her.

"Alex," she murmured against his lips. She moved backward; he followed her, again capturing her mouth with his own, drunk on whatever it was that he'd found on her lips, whatever it was that was driving him mad.

After a few heady seconds, she pulled back again, and with a deeper regret than he'd ever known, he let her. "Alex, I can't do this." He noticed she couldn't quite meet his eyes.

God, she must think he was an idiot, attacking her like that after she'd obviously been through something awful.

"I'm sorry." She twisted her slim hands together, examining the chunky silver ring on her index finger. "We barely know each other. I really shouldn't—"

He placed his fingertips under her chin and gently lifted, so her dark blue eyes met his, and her lips parted slightly. This time, she didn't pull away from him, but rather seemed to lean slightly into him, as if she didn't want him to stop. He didn't want to stop.

He knew so little about her, and what she'd told him he went back and forth on, doubting her words were true. But the chemistry between them hit him like a freight train every time he touched her. And he couldn't seem to stop touching her. "No, *I'm* sorry." Thankfully, his voice was steady when he spoke, instead of cracking like that of the hormone-driven middle schooler he'd obviously been channeling. "I thought—" He dropped his hand, backed away to give her some space. "I thought something had happened to you."

Her hands fumbled for the lapels of her sweater, and she pulled them together, just below her collarbone. "It almost did."

"Tell me."

She'd piled her reddish-brown curls on top of her

head, giving her the look of an Irish goddess, but a few had escaped around her temple, and he fought off the urge to capture one between his fingers. As a few miscellaneous cops strode past them, careful to give the two of them a wide berth, Sophie relayed what had happened that evening, from the note she'd found on the car to the intruder who'd broken in to her apartment. And before she'd finished, Alex found himself dying to punch something.

Starting, preferably, with his father.

The hallway opened up like a balcony toward the interior of the complex, similar in style to a fancy hotel he'd stayed in once. He moved toward the edge, palming the cool brass railing as he stared at the bustle of curious residents and grim-faced cops in the courtyard below. "I'm sorry, Sophie," he murmured.

He felt her move up beside him. "It's not your fault. You're not controlling him."

But somehow it was his fault. He was, after all, the common denominator in the attempt on his mother's life and the near-attack on Sophie. "You said the guy who broke in to your apartment suddenly left. Any idea why?" He desperately wanted to believe that Jack Runningwater hadn't intended to hurt Sophie, but the fact that his mother was lying in a hospital bed and Sophie's butcher knives had been found in disarray on her counter instead of carefully put away as she'd left them belied that.

She reached up and tugged absentmindedly at a

freckled earlobe as she, too, watched the people on the ground floor. "I'm not sure. I had nowhere to go, so I went and hid in my closet, behind my clothes. I thought maybe I could surprise him when he opened it by hitting him with the lamp."

It was pretty much the worst self-defense plan he'd ever heard in his life, but given that Sophie's apartment was on the eighth floor and she'd had no weapons or phones near her, he guessed that had probably been the best she could have done. Before he let her sleep alone there again, he'd take her shopping for a few things, including a stun gun and a pay-as-you-go cell phone. "So did you? Hit him?"

"No. He opened the closet door, and then he just,,,left. I think he might have heard something." She sighed and began twisting her ring around and around her finger. "What I don't understand is why he didn't even give me time to follow his stupid warning. I get the note, I go home, he comes after me. It makes no sense." She explained the note, which she'd already given to the cops. She was right—none of it made sense.

Behind them, someone close by cleared his throat, and Alex looked over his shoulder to see Aaron Donovan approaching. Sophie sidestepped away from Alex, an interesting blush tinting her cheeks. Pulling her hands into the sleeves of her sweater, she tucked them under her chin as if she were trying to fold into herself.

He nodded at Aaron in greeting. "Donovan."

"Alex. I'm glad you're here, even though we got cut off earlier." The detective pivoted to include Sophie in the conversation. "Ms. Brennan asked us to call you."

Sophie squinched her eyes shut briefly, baring her teeth at him in an embarrassed grimace. "I was a little hysterical. I never would have dragged you away from your mom if I'd been thinking."

There seemed to be a lot of that going around. "It's okay, Soph. I'm glad you had them call me."

"We would have wanted to talk with you anyway," Aaron said, probably including his partner, Eddie Ventaglia, in that "we." He glanced at Sophie, clearly wondering if he should talk about family matters in front of her.

"Can I go back into my apartment now?" she asked, deftly picking up on Aaron's vibe. "I could use some coffee. You two like some?" Both of them nodded, and she ducked inside her half-open doorway.

Aaron rubbed the stubble on his chin, his expression thoughtful. It was well past midnight, and Alex could tell from the state of his post-five-o'clock shadow and the rumpled state of his suit that the man's shift had probably ended hours ago. "So. Can you think of any reason why your father would go after Sophie?"

"He's been corrupted by the power of the Dark Side?" At Aaron's answering scowl, he shrugged. "Dude. I haven't seen the man since I was six."

"Anything your mother may have told you about him that didn't have to do with George Lucas?"

Alex rolled his eyes. "My mother doesn't talk about him. Ever. But no, I have no clue." He thought of all the basketball games with only one parent on the sidelines, the other boys who'd had fathers to shoot hoops with in the off season, the annual father-son athletic club dinners he'd always skipped, and he wanted to punch his old man all over again. Alex thought he'd dealt with his so-called abandonment issues a long time ago, but all of this brought it back, as if he were six again. "So suddenly, he comes around after all these years and goes after my mother?" He hit the wall with the side of his fist and paced over to the short wall overlooking the courtyard. "It makes zero sense to me. Plus, the one thing my mother did tell me was that she doesn't think he killed anyone. Including Wilma Red Cloud."

Aaron nodded grimly.

"Either way, what connection Mom and I have to the guy I found in the woods, I have no clue." He put his hands on the railing and looked down. Most of the residents had gone back to their rooms, and now only the occasional cop walked through the courtyard. "And how Sophie fits into all of this…?"

Moving up to join Alex at the railing, Aaron leaned back against it, folding his arms. "She might be the real thing, Al."

"How's that?"

"We checked her out," Aaron explained. "Apparently, the police in her hometown of Grant's Pass, Oregon, seem to think she's as psychic as she claims."

Slanting a glance at his friend, Alex found himself confronting his skepticism head-on once more. It was one thing for him to entertain the possibility that Sophie had more than just a really strong intuitive bent. But law enforcement doing so? "Oh, really?"

"Don't look at me like that. Apparently, she's called in with tips on a few unrelated missing persons' cases." He hitched up a shoulder in a strange little half shrug. "The detective I talked to told me she was always on the money. And may have saved more than a few lives."

"And you believe them?" Alex asked.

"They're cops. They don't get all woo-woo…" Aaron made finger quotes in the air "—unless there's a good reason."

Ever since he'd met Sophie, Alex had been struggling to piece together a logical, real-world explanation for how she had known about the body in the woods, how she'd seemed to know about his deceased aunt Polly, how she'd oh-so-casually tossed out the loaded phrase *Crow Carrier* at him. And in his mind he had, but the theory that she was insane and in league with his father lost credibility every time he talked to her. There was nothing vicious about Sophie Brennan, he'd bet his life on it.

Then she'd done the impossible, predicting that

his mother would need to dodge a bullet as soon as she started speaking about "yellow birds." Even if Sophie had somehow been in league with the shooter, there was no way she could have timed her prediction to pan out as it had. He knew that, but he hadn't been ready to do much more than simply put the whole thing out of his head—until Aaron, one of the most logical people he knew, told him that it just might be possible.

"Oh, hey," Aaron broke in to his thoughts. "There's one more thing. Apparently you can't ask her questions from the beyond. She has to come to you, or…"

He couldn't contain the wry grin that spread across his face. "Or she sucks." That was Sophie, all right.

"You got it."

At that moment, Sophie came back through the door, holding two mugs filled with steaming coffee. She handed one to each of them, then ducked back to retrieve one more for herself. "Don't worry. I totally didn't hear you talking about me." She carefully sipped her coffee, smirking at him over the top of the mug. He tried his best not to squirm uncomfortably under her gaze.

"So, Detective." She turned to Aaron. "Have you two come up with any ideas as to why this happened? I mean, my first impulse is to believe that someone broke in to my apartment intending to rob me. But it's too much of a coincidence—Alex's mother, the note and now this. Not to mention the body in the woods."

"Actually, about that body…" Reaching inside his jacket, Aaron pulled a small notebook out of the inner breast pocket. "We got an ID earlier today. One Charles Franklin, age sixty-three, executive board member of the Centrix Corporation. Ring any bells?"

Well, that was a shock. Just when everything was starting to come together in the smallest way, good old Dad threw them all for a loop. "No bells here."

Sophie shook her head. "No. I've never heard of him. Or of Centrix. What do they do?"

Aaron flipped back a couple of pages in his notebook. "They manufacture industrial-strength cleaners and petroleum-based plastics. Before we came here, we were at their headquarters in Seattle interviewing some of the executives who've been with the company for a long time." His mouth flattened into a frustrated line. "They all said they'd never heard of your father, Alex."

"Without being able to talk to Mom, I don't think I'm going to be much help coming up with a connection, either." He felt the now-familiar twist in his gut as he recalled the situation in which he'd left his mother.

"Right. Well…" Putting the notebook back in his pocket, Aaron turned to Sophie. "We interviewed all of your neighbors. Most of them were asleep when your visitor came, and none of them heard or saw anything, unfortunately."

"What, Millie wasn't at your door, guns blazing?" Alex interjected. "I would've thought she and the Neighborhood Watch would be on top of it."

He'd meant it as a joke, but Sophie wasn't laughing. Her eyes opened wide and she inhaled sharply. "Millie? Oh, my God, I didn't even—Detective, did you speak to my neighbor on this side?" She gestured toward the apartment on the far side of hers.

Aaron shook his head. "No, she didn't answer our knock. We figured we'd try again later."

"Millie had watch duty tonight. There's no way she wouldn't have " Sophie trailed off, bolting forward toward Millie's front door. Before they could stop her, she'd yanked it open, though Aaron managed to clamp a hand on her shoulder and pull her back before she could step inside, his other hand hovering over his holster.

But Sophie had seen something in that apartment, something that had washed all the color from her already fair skin. As she stumbled back, Alex put out his hands to catch her, and when he did, he could feel her trembling violently.

"Oh, Millie. Oh, no."

Chapter Seven

Sophie couldn't hold back the tears when the Port Renegade EMTs wheeled Millie's sheet-covered body out of her apartment and into the hallway. The last few hours since they'd discovered Millie's body, her head twisted at a horrible angle and her lifeless eyes just staring upward, had passed by in a blur of cops, questions and long periods of silence. Sophie had thought she was too numb to feel anything anymore. But watching Millie leave her home for the last time…Sophie couldn't help but think of her family, about how they'd have to live forever with the knowledge that they'd lost their mother and grandmother in a violent, senseless way.

She felt Alex approach her—knowing even though she didn't turn around that it was him. He enveloped her from behind in his arms, and she allowed herself to lean back against him and accept the solace he offered, placing one of her hands over his clasped ones. "I know she was mean to you when you first met her, but Millie was actually a really amazing woman." Her breath caught on every word, making her sentence choppy and halted. "She was eighty-seven, and she had so much energy."

"Yeah, she was quite a force," Alex agreed, his cheek warm and rough against hers. She didn't know how long this would last, his presence here, but she was grateful for it all the same.

"I had the flu earlier this year, and she came over with chicken broth and didn't leave until she'd cleaned my entire apartment." Sophie smiled at the memory of the elderly woman's relentless kindness, until the realization that she wouldn't see Millie ever again suddenly seemed to suck all the air out of the room. "This is so unfair. She didn't deserve this."

"No. She didn't." She knew he was blaming himself and she wished she could comfort him, but she didn't know what to say. There weren't words in any language that would make the situation better.

Aaron had told them that it appeared that Millie had probably poked her head out of her apartment when she'd heard someone at Sophie's door. Knowing the woman as she did, she knew that Millie would have started interrogating the intruder immediately—and he'd shoved her back inside and had easily overpowered her. According to Aaron and his partner, the bruises on her jaw seemed to indicate that she'd been pistol-whipped, hard enough to break her fragile neck and kill her instantly.

Looking more than a little worse for wear, his shirttail hanging out on one side and his curly dark hair dancing about his head in frightening disarray, Detective Ventaglia came out of Millie's apartment and made a determined beeline for the two of them.

"Hey, Ms. Brennan." She'd heard him barking orders at the beat cops around him all night, but his rumbling bass grew gentle whenever he spoke to her. "I think we have all we need from the two of you. You can head home if you want."

Her eyes darted to her apartment door, and suddenly the very last thing she wanted to do was go inside and try to sleep in that big empty place alone, with Millie's too-empty apartment just a thin wall away.

"Do you have someplace else to go?" the detective asked, apparently rather gifted at reading facial ticks. "Me, I wouldn't want to sleep alone in there either."

"I'll be—" *Fine. Say it. You'll be fine. It's not like you have anyplace else to go.*

"She can come home with me."

Sophie jerked her head to stare at Alex, and he just looked back with his jaw clenched tightly and his brown eyes narrowed, as if daring her to challenge his plan. But frankly, she was just too tired to do anything but acquiesce. Lacing her fingers together, she stretched her arms in front of her and stifled a yawn. "Okay," she agreed.

"Okay." Alex nodded once, confirming the plan. And suddenly all the adrenaline that had been fueling her for half the night seemed to seep out of her body, leaving her limbs thick and ponderous and her head feeling as if it were too big and too heavy to hold up. Staying on her feet was about all she could manage right now.

"That's a great idea," Ventaglia responded. "Hey, we sent a patrol to check out your house not too long ago. One of your windows was open a crack, but nothing looked out of place. I'll send someone home with you to make sure everything is okay, and we'll have officers driving by as often as we can spare them until this whole thing goes away."

Goes away. Whenever that would be. "Mmm-hmm," she said in a feeble attempt to prove that despite her undoubtedly slack-jawed expression, she was paying attention.

She vaguely registered the rest of Alex's conversation with Eddie, and then promptly forgot it in the effort to store up enough energy to make it out to the parking lot on her own steam. After helping her pack up a few things, Alex let her lean on him, helping her into his truck. She must've fallen asleep shortly thereafter because the next thing she knew, they were in front of a big brown house, and he was trying to lift her out.

"Stop that," she murmured. "You'll burst something if you try to lift me." She hopped out of the pickup, so eager for a warm bed and a cozy blanket, she was practically shaking.

"You?" Alex scoffed. "You're tiny." She didn't

want to give him a chance to prove her right, so she put one foot in front of the other, heading for the outside staircase that would take them above the garage level to the second main floor. Despite her determination to make it up on her own, she felt him put an arm around her and suddenly the climb got easier. Once inside, she glanced at the room and its strange lack of functional furniture, and dismissed it all as unimportant. "Bed?"

He chuckled softly beside her. "This way, madame." He said something to the cop who'd followed them and led her up to the third floor.

And then finally, thankfully, she was lying on a very large, very soft mattress, with beautiful white sheets that felt like silk underneath her cheek. She kicked off her shoes, and he unbuttoned her coat and helped her out of it, and then, as she sank into the softness of his bed and closed her eyes, he pulled a blanket over her and tucked it around her shoulders.

The room grew quiet then, and she thought he had gone. But then she realized that she could still hear him breathing.

"Good night, beautiful," he whispered.

With that, Sophie felt herself drifting off to sleep with a smile on her face, too exhausted to protest Alex's lie about her looks.

WHEN SHE FINALLY AWOKE, late in the morning judging by the quantity of sunlight bombarding her through the window, it took Sophie a few seconds to remember where she was. In fact, the bed felt so soft and the sheets were of such great quality, she was almost tempted to sink back into them and let herself drift off once again, with the smell of his soap lingering on the fabric beneath her. But then she remembered that she was in Alex Gray's house.

And he'd called her beautiful.

The recollection was enough to send a zinging spark of energy all through her, and suddenly she just wanted to see him. Out of her league or not, with his intensely good-looking face and billboard-quality body, she wanted to see him. A girl could dream, right?

And oh, how she'd dreamed.

Of the feel of his hands in places they'd never been, and the sound of his voice telling her things he'd never spoken to her, of the way her body felt as if it were blooming whenever he touched her, even if just casually. It was all grossly inappropriate, considering everything that had happened, considering her poor, poor neighbor's fate. But all the same, she had to see him.

Running her fingers through her tangled, curly hair, she padded to the door and pulled it open.

Wow, she really hadn't dreamed the lack of furniture in this place. Alex's house boasted huge windows, a spectacular view and the most beautiful gleaming cherry floors she'd ever seen. But he really needed to invest in some furnishings that didn't have past lives as shipping crates or storage bins.

In one corner of the living room sat the ugliest recliner she'd ever seen, upholstered in a nubby brown fabric that may have been in fashion circa 1987. Being a guy, he'd parked that abomination in front of a television the size of a minivan, accompanied, of course, by a state-of-the-art stereo system. Obviously, Alex's decorating priorities lay with having the best TV money could buy and a really great bed. She didn't even want to think about whether that was because he wanted a good night's sleep—or something else.

A nice little antique dining-room table with four matching chairs sat behind the recliner in the breakfast nook. And a variety of colorful plastic milk crates dotted the rest of the space, serving as end tables, spare seating and even, in one case, a coatrack.

An amazing view of the snowcapped Olympic Mountains, visible through an entire wall of windows, more than made up for the lack of furniture, however.

Entranced by the mountains, as well as the stretch of snow-covered grass and evergreen trees in the yard that, through a trick of perspective, seemed to lead right up to them, Sophie didn't notice that Alex was awake until he cleared his throat behind her.

She turned and noticed him sitting in one of the four chairs surrounding the antique table in the breakfast nook, his hands resting on the keys of a laptop—state of the art, naturally. If he put as much effort into choosing the furniture as he did into selecting electronics, the house would immediately go from amazing to wow.

"Hey." His black hair glistened with moisture, and the clean scent of a no-nonsense soap filled her nostrils as she moved toward him. Her hand floated up instinctively to tug through her hair, although she knew that without conditioner and some serious anti-frizz serum, it was a lost cause at the moment. But then she realized that he wasn't even paying attention to the frightening state of her hair or to her presence in general—he had eyes solely for his laptop screen.

While she debated whether to ask him what he was looking at, he pushed the chair back, the legs skidding noisily against the wood floors, and stood. His mouth was set in a grim line and his dark eyes had a hollow look to them, as if he'd taken some strong emotions and had buried them deep. "Take a look at this." He spun the laptop around to face her.

Second Centrix Executive Found Murdered.

She squinted at the screen, leaning forward so she could see the rest of the *Seattle Times* article, a brilliant red Breaking News banner scrolling at the top of it. "Second? You mean…?"

"There's been another murder, yeah." He scratched his hands vigorously along his scalp, something she noticed he did when anything bothered him.

She braced her hands on the back of one of the dining chairs. "Last night?"

"They found the body a couple of hours ago, according to this." He smacked the back of the laptop screen, causing it to tilt forward slightly so the words were no longer visible to her. "Same method—strangled with a garrote and then left covered with a sheet with a nice pretty picture stabbed into his chest." Alex folded his arms across his chest, the muscles in them bunching so a few veins stood out in relief. To any bystander he'd look perfectly calm, sound perfectly reasonable, but the anger and…shame came off him like a black whirlwind of emotion that she could almost reach out and touch. She wanted to tell him that it would all be okay, that they'd catch the man responsible for all of this and that his mother would wake up and be fine. But it would be ridiculous to promise all of that, so she kept her mouth shut.

"Dad's getting bolder," Alex continued in a monotone. "He left this guy right in the main parking lot of the Centrix compound."

It wasn't a kind visual, and she supposed it was even worse for him, since he'd found the initial body and had seen the killer's handiwork firsthand.

"The article didn't mention the crow feather," he said. "I had to call Aaron this morning to confirm that it was there."

"Crow feather?" She had no idea what he was talking about, although she had a nagging feeling that it should make sense to her.

His eyes clouded, and though he was looking right at her, she knew he couldn't see her. He walked over to the wall of windows and stared out at the horizon, where the snowcapped Olympics met the crisp blue morning sky. "My father's calling card. The first body had one in its right hand. So did Wilma Red Cloud."

Crow Carrier. A strong gust of wind hit the house, rattling the windows and whipping the tall thin trees outdoors from side to side, and it seemed to carry the words right to her. "A crow feather," she murmured, considering the possibilities.

A corner of his mouth quirked upward. "The crow carrier. You really hit something when you called me that the other day at the hospital." He bent his head, looking down at his bare feet peeking out of the frayed hems of his jeans.

"Interestingly enough, even though I said it, I have no idea what it means." It was a lame attempt at lightening up the conversation, but his face softened all the same.

"That's one thing my mother did tell me. Back in what she calls 'the buffalo days,' the Oglala men divided themselves into warrior societies. My ancestors were *kangi'yuha,* or crow carriers." His eyes darted around, and Sophie had the distinct impression that he was waiting for someone to jump out and tell him he had his facts wrong. "They were the skilled, proven warriors, and they wore crow feathers and even stuffed crows around their necks when they went into battle to help their arrows fly true."

Now it all made sense. Thank goodness she hadn't inadvertently insulted him when she'd come up with that phrase out of nowhere. "So the crow feather is his way of marking his conquests. He sees his victims as adversaries in battle?"

"Damn if I know," Alex scoffed. He turned around and leaned his forehead on the glass, and she moved up beside him, wondering how she could offer him comfort, wondering if you could possibly comfort someone in a situation like this.

"Can you read his mind, Soph?" He made a fist and tapped it against the glass, a light touch, but one filled with pent-up frustration. "Can you tell me what the hell he's thinking? Because I don't know him. He's my father, and I don't remember a damned thing."

She'd become so used to the constant undercurrent of skepticism coloring their every interaction that his questions startled her, to say the least. And, unfortunately, they had the inevitable effect of slamming a steel door on all things metaphysical. Anytime she actually *tried* to get a read on something, she not only failed miserably, but it usually stifled any preternatural ability she had for days, even weeks. But she found herself trying anyway, concentrating on the shadowy figure in her mind that was Jack Runningwater.

And pretty much came up with a nice mental picture of a Native American actor who had been in a lot of B movies in the last decade.

Wiping the actor out of her head, she stared out at the mountains and tried again, relaxing her body and letting her eyelids grow heavy and her vision blur.

This time, she got Kevin Costner in the old Academy Award winner *Dances with Wolves*, making buffalo horns on his head with his fingers and trying to pronounce *tatanka*.

"I'm sorry. I don't—" Without thinking, she put her hand on his bicep and something shot up her arm that was more than just the usual one-sided chemistry she felt around him.

"The attack on your mother…" *Don't think. Just talk.* "And on Millie and me, seem cold to me, targeted. Like someone's going after something, and we're all in the way." She kept her hand on him, knowing that she probably looked like a big dork to him but afraid to lose her train of thought. "But these Centrix murders feel almost…hot. There's passion behind them, revenge. It's almost as if two different people are working here."

"Maybe Dad acquired a couple of new personalities while he's been away." Alex bent his head to look at her, and their faces were so close, Sophie had to back away or she'd reveal way too much.

But just when she broke contact, his hand shot

up and covered hers, pressing it once more against the bare skin of his arm. She blinked at him, wondering what had possessed him to do that.

"You seem to get some kind of clarity when you touch me," he murmured, his deep voice wrapping around her like the silken sheets in his bed.

She dropped her eyes, focusing on his hand as a tide of warmth rushed up her entire body. She knew her face had undoubtedly turned fire-engine red, and it didn't take a psychic to realize that the energy in the room had abruptly changed. The phrase *ladies' man* bounced around in her mind like a Ping-Pong ball in zero gravity.

"You okay, Soph?"

"You're flirting with me," she informed his hand.

"Really?" His voice was teasing, and it just made her blush even more. She could enjoy this, appreciate the fact that she could distract him from his hurt, but she couldn't.

"It's like second nature to you. You don't even think about what you're saying."

Pivoting his body to face her head-on, he still didn't let go of her hand. "I know exactly what I'm saying, beautiful." He wasn't laughing anymore. And she still couldn't look at him.

She tried to pull her hand away, but he wouldn't loosen his grip, so she tugged harder, until she managed to free herself, her arm swinging back once he let her go. "Don't call me that."

He arched an eyebrow. "Why not?"

The surge of annoyance mingled with embarrassment finally gave her the strength to look him in the eye. "Because you're mocking me. Guys like you don't look at women like me."

He cocked his head slightly to the side and shot her a bemused look.

"Women who wear a size in the double digits." She smacked her palms lightly against her admittedly full hips, curling her lips at the fullness of her thighs. Someday, she really was going to have to make getting to the gym four or five times a week a priority. "You know, women who aren't about to diet themselves invisible." *Shut up, shut up, shut up.* But unfortunately, she'd thrown all that out there, and now she couldn't seem to stop sounding like a giant bundle of neediness with feet.

He smothered a laugh as his gaze traveled up and down her body, and his amusement coupled with his scrutiny just made her want to mummify herself in five more oversize cardigans like the one she wore. Either that or wrap the one she had around his head and make a run for it.

As it was, she didn't think she could be any more mortified. And wallowing in that embarrassment prevented her from sensing his next move, so he took her by surprise when he closed the space between them. His eyelids lowered as a slow, seductive smile spread across his too-handsome face.

"I'm looking at you, Sophie," he murmured. "And I am most definitely not mocking you." His mouth so close to hers, all she'd have had to do was raise herself up on her toes, and…

"Shut up, I'm not your type. Guys like you—" She couldn't breathe; she could barely think, and the fact made her attempt at rebuffing him just sound breathless and unconvincing. God, she felt as if she were drunk, just because a good-looking man was flirting with her. How sad was that?

She took a step back, hoping to break the spell he had her under by putting some distance between them, but she merely ended up with her back against the wall. And now there was nowhere to run.

"And what are guys like me?" His nearness forced her to look up to keep eye contact with him, and her pulse went into triple time as a result. He was close. So close, she was breathing in the very air he exhaled. Oh, mama, this was so not good. Because while she'd always been good at interpreting the most subtle signals people put out, she knew there was nothing subtle about her reaction to Alex Gray. Her entire body felt flushed, hot, and almost boneless—another minute of this and she'd probably spontaneously combust, in case he had any doubt of his effect on her.

She schooled her features into the most blasé expression she could manage, under the circumstances. "Come on, Alex. You know what you look like."

He bared his teeth at her in a cocky grin that looked decidedly vulpine. "No, what do I look like?"

She swallowed, trying to buy time, and then

decided that brutal honesty was her best policy. "You look like a guy who has no trouble getting any woman he wants."

He dipped his head, and was he actually nuzzling her neck? She flattened her palms against the wall, pushing against it in an intense effort to keep from sinking to the floor. "And you, Sophie Brennan—" she could feel his lips moving against the tender skin at her throat "—look like a goddess."

With that, he rose upward, his mouth brushing softly against her hers, and she wished time could stop, so she could feel this beautiful and this desired for just a little longer. She closed her eyes, running a palm against his rock-hard chest, dying for him to really kiss her, terrified that he would.

"Don't," she whispered, then clenched her fingers to grab a fistful of his shirt.

He straightened, blowing out a forceful breath as he obviously tried to switch gears, but he didn't back away. "Sure," he said, "but you're sending me mixed messages here." He glanced pointedly at where she clung to his shirt. "What's it gonna be, Soph?"

What's it gonna be? Good question, and one to which she didn't have an answer. At least, not one that made sense.

The shrill sound of the doorbell felt like a cold, wet blanket of sanity smacking her in the face, and she ducked underneath his arm and darted away from him. "Better get that. Might be important." She headed for the laptop and made a big show of casually scrolling through the article about the second Centrix murder.

Behind her, he was silent for what seemed like a very long stretch of time. The doorbell rang again. She heard him head for the door and undo the locks when he got to it.

"Well, hello, lover," a smoky female voice intoned. Sophie couldn't help but turn her head to get a glimpse of the speaker. Calling someone *lover* seemed awkward and strange, but for some reason, the woman at the door pulled it off, making it a natural and disturbingly intimate way to address someone who had just had Sophie up against a wall….

He didn't have *you against anything. Because you were too scared to even go there.*

Over Alex's shoulder, she caught a glimpse of glossy, stick-straight blond hair, the kind she wished for every time she woke up and looked as if she'd taken a pizza cutter and a food processor to her curly hair. Abandoning all pretense of reading the article, she sidestepped to the left, getting a perfect view of the tight aqua sweater that accentuated the blonde's tiny waist and flat stomach.

"I was in town, and I thought I'd see if you were home. I'm so glad they don't have you working on a Sunday this time." The woman reached up to put her arms around Alex's neck, but he stepped back in time to avoid her.

"Uh, hey, Amanda. Now isn't really a good—"

That was when Amanda noticed Sophie staring at them. Ignoring Alex for the moment, she came inside, dragging a small wheeled travel bag with the American Airlines logo on it behind her, a strange little smile on her flawlessly made-up face. "Oh, hello. Who is this, your new girlfriend?" Setting the suitcase on its end, she stretched her manicured hand out. Though it hung there limply as if she expected Sophie to kiss her rings rather than shake it, Sophie opted for the latter.

"Nice to meet you," Sophie said automatically.

Alex shuffled his weight from foot to foot. "Yeah, so, anyway Amanda—"

"Well, you're a refreshing change from his usual type," Amanda singsonged, making it clear that change was not a good thing in this case.

There was only one way to put a stop to this idiotic conversation. "I'm not his girlfriend. Really."

Amanda flashed her veneers at Sophie. "Oh, great. So you wouldn't mind—"

"Oooookay." Gripping Amanda's arm, Alex steered her to the other side of the kitchen, where a set of glass doors opened out onto the patio. "We need to talk. Now."

Sophie wondered if she should take advantage of the moment to gather her things and leave quietly, but then Alex poked his head back through the doors. "And don't you go anywhere." He closed them with a whoosh and she sat down, idly playing with the laptop's mouse pad.

Though the closed doors muffled the conversation so she couldn't make out a thing they said, she knew that whatever was going on between them wasn't good. By the sound of things, Alex seemed to be keeping his cool, but Amanda grew louder and more shrill each second. When Sophie braved a glance over the top of the laptop screen, she saw Amanda swiping at her eyes with the back of her hand. Alex tried to touch her arm, but she yanked it away and started yelling again.

Finally, she strode to the patio doors and pulled them open. "Have fun with your fat girlfriend!" she shouted over her shoulder and then entered the house, closing the door on Alex behind her.

Sophie stood up, not quite knowing what to say. Goodbye? Great to meet you? Go have a doughnut before you start to resemble a human PEZ dispenser? But then Amanda stumbled and brought herself up short, as if she'd just realized that Sophie had heard her.

"Oh." She put her hand over her mouth, speaking through her fingers. "I'm so sorry. I didn't mean…"

Sophie raised her own hand, palm outward, to stop whatever lame apology Amanda was about to utter.

But then the stewardess seemed to shrink several inches as she let her shoulders slump, and her pink-glossed bottom lip quivered. "I'm just really, really jealous. I've been in love with that jerk for years now."

Sophie didn't know how to respond to that, so she just wrinkled her forehead in what she hoped passed for sympathy.

Tilting her head to indicate her travel bag, Amanda grabbed the handle and kicked the small suitcase back so it was in prime rolling position. "Come to see him every time American puts me on the Tulsa-Seattle schedule. Maybe it's time to take that nonstop to Honolulu now." She made her way to the door and pulled it open.

"I'm really sorry," Sophie said, suddenly wanting to make everything a little bit better for Amanda. She noticed that Alex had wisely stayed behind closed doors on the patio. "There isn't any reason for you to be jealous, though."

Amanda sniffed, giving her a sad little smile. "You know, you seem like a nice girl. You don't want to mess with him. He's a player with a capital *P*." She pulled her bag outside and closed the door softly behind her.

Feeling suddenly worn out, Sophie wandered into the living room and sat down in Alex's recliner, staring at the giant expanse of gray glass that was the television screen. She heard the patio doors slide open, then shut, and then Alex walked into the room. She didn't look at him—she couldn't—so he sat down on the arm of her chair.

After a few seconds of silence, he finally spoke. "I'm sorry about that."

She shook her head. "No need. It's your life."

She shuffled to the opposite side of the chair so she could look at him without feeling as if he were on top of her. "Felt a little sorry for Amanda, though."

He hitched a shoulder upward. "I haven't seen her in ages. I'm not sure why she showed up like that out of the blue."

"She said she's in love with you."

He laughed softly. "Amanda is in love with shoes, flying and loving and leaving men in every city. Not necessarily in that order."

She couldn't help herself. "And this is the kind of woman you choose to date?"

He grimaced. "I wouldn't exactly say we dated…."

Pushing off the chair with her hands, Sophie rose and walked across the room. "I don't want to hear this."

He followed her, putting his hands on her arms and turning her gently to face him. "It was a long time ago. I'm sorry she upset you."

"I'm fine."

He gave her a slow, lazy half smile. "Yes, you are fine."

She smacked her palms against his chest and shoved, causing him to stumble back, a look of surprise on his face. "See, that's what you do. You go through life on the surface, flirting and being charming, and making everyone love you because you're funny and cute and the life of the party. But when it comes to things that are real, you can't handle it. If we got involved, you'd run, because

I don't have a plane to catch or another party to go to."

Now it was his turn to flush. He jabbed a finger at her and opened his mouth to speak, but she stopped him with her words.

"I get hits off of people, and I'm never, *ever* wrong. And I could read you like a book the first time I met you," she snapped at him. Somewhere far off in the distance, she could feel the real Sophie floating above the conversation, watching her furious doppelgänger do something really, really stupid. But she couldn't seem to stop.

He closed his mouth and just stared at her for a moment, and when he did speak, he was deadly quiet. "Oh, really? And what did you see, Sophie Brennan, that scared you so much?"

"You don't scare me."

In two steps, he was directly in front of her, so close he had to look down to see her. "Tell me you don't feel this." He grabbed her hand and put it on his chest, and just that small contact nearly made her lose her mind all over again.

She swallowed, all of her misplaced anger melting away and leaving her feeling small. And scared. Instead of denying it, she dismissed it. "It doesn't matter."

"Why?"

Such a simple question, and it had such a complicated answer. She flipped a palm in the air, struggling to find her conversational footing once more.

Backing away, he shoved his hands in the front pockets of his jeans. She could feel the pent-up energy coming off him in waves, and the air between them suddenly caught fire. Again.

He's out of your league, honey. She could just hear her mother.

"Because I know you better than you think, Alex Gray." Out. She had to get out, get away from him. She stumbled toward the front door, turning only after she had her hand around the cool solidness of the steel knob. "You know, you're right, every time I touch you, I do get clarity. And I know beyond the shadow of a doubt that if I let myself fall for you, you're going to break my heart."

Chapter Eight

In an awkward but necessary move, Sophie had managed to catch Amanda before she drove away in her rental car and had persuaded the woman to give her a lift to the UW library and, more importantly, away from Alex's house. Actually, it hadn't taken much persuasion, as Amanda seemed to be eager to make amends for the "fat girlfriend" comment and even more eager to have someone to listen to her rant about Alex's "emotional unavailability" and "deep-seated narcissism."

Once at the library, having been politely noncommittal when Amanda called out from her car that they should "do this again sometime," Sophie tried to work on the term paper she had due on Monday. But her thoughts kept returning to Alex, and when she wasn't practically going up in flames remembering what it felt like when he'd kissed her, she thought about Millie, which just felt awful.

Do something. You have to do something.

But she'd never felt more useless and helpless in her life. Millie was dead, and Sophie hadn't seen it coming. Alex's mother was lying unconscious in a hospital bed, and she hadn't had a clue. Every time she tried to consider the near future and what it held for her, for Alex, for everyone embroiled in this strange chain reaction of violence, she came up with the same result: nothing.

Fat lot of good it did being marginally psychic. All her ability seemed to do was rear its ugly head just in time to freak people out and prevent them from wanting to be her friend—or more. She didn't know how many daily masses her mother had attended when Sophie had been younger and still living at home—all because something Sophie had said or predicted had frightened her. Nothing like being thought a devil child to get a teenager to strike out on her own as soon as humanly possible. Sure, she knew her mother loved her, but always with the possibility that Sophie could and should change foremost in her mind, in a million different ways.

Propping her elbow on the four-person table she had all to herself, she rubbed her forehead and then just let it rest in her hand. She'd been staring at the same Degas biography for, oh, about two hours now, and it was getting her nowhere.

Do something.

She slipped her hand under the front cover and smacked the heavy book shut, the loud thud the pages made when they slapped together causing a few heads to turn in her direction. She gave her fellow students an apologetic shrug, then glanced over at the cluster of library computers on the other side of the wing in which she sat.

If Alex Gray insisted on popping into her thoughts every five minutes, then she'd have to take action to exorcise him, or take a failing grade on her paper as a result of her less-than-stellar study habits. Leaving her stack of books on the table to save her spot, she moved to one of the empty computers and scanned her student ID through the card reader to get on the library's Internet account. Art-history students probably weren't experts when it came to researching twentieth-century non-art-related events, but she did have access to LexisNexis, which would do the searching through most U.S. newspapers for her.

"Let's see…." Normally, she didn't talk to herself, but the library was fairly empty—probably due to the cold weather and the fact that it was Sunday. She felt a pang of guilt at skipping church, knowing her mother would definitely not approve, especially if she knew Sophie hadn't slept in her own apartment last night. "All major U.S. newspapers." She clicked her mouse on the appropriate box. "All dates." When the search box finally appeared on the screen, she typed the words *Pine Woods Reservation,* where she'd long ago learned that Wilma Red Cloud had lived, *Centrix* and, on a hunch, *crow carrier,* then set the specialized search engine running.

It only took her fifteen minutes and three articles before she knew she was on to something huge.

She spent the better part of the day running back and forth from the computer to the printing center to pay for what ended up being a healthy stack of copies. When she finally pushed through the library doors, crisp, cold air blasted her in the face, a sensation that almost surprised her, since an entire day of sitting under fluorescent lights made her feel as if she hadn't been outside in about a year.

The sky was a mixture of brilliant orange, pink and purple, the position of the sun telling her she had less than half an hour before it grew dark—and the last thing she wanted was to be in the dark alone. Fortunately, the walk to Sunnyside View from the library was a short one. She dumped her stack of printouts in the passenger seat of her car, which sat just as she'd left it on the far side of the parking lot because Millie had once suggested that she leave the closer spots for her older and often less mobile neighbors.

Millie.

Oh, God, she was never going to get the image of that poor woman's broken body and dead, staring eyes out of her mind. Of all the times when her psychic impulses went awry, why couldn't they kick in now? Why couldn't she just know where Millie's murderer was? Why couldn't the key to capturing him just come to her, so she could tell the police and they could all breathe a little easier?

Of course, whoever had killed Millie had probably been looking for Sophie. But why? She had no doubt last night's break-in was tied to Alex, whether the police had reached that conclusion or not.

She went around to the driver's side and got in, pushing the button to lock herself inside. She didn't want to let last night's break-in scare her so much she was afraid to be alone even in broad daylight in a fairly public parking lot, but it did. And she couldn't help but feel as though there were eyes watching from every shadowy corner around the building. What was the motive? Why would someone come looking for her?

He's looking for something.

The thought came from out of nowhere, as if someone else had whispered it inside her head, but it made sense. Her would-be attacker hadn't broken in to her place and immediately gone after her, like your average Joe Serial Killer would have. He'd moved around the main area outside her bedroom. She'd heard him shuffling papers.

And if he was looking for something and it was tied to Alex, chances were that he was going to need to search Alex's house, too. In fact, that might have been his primary objective from the beginning.

A prickling, clammy sense of unease crawled across her skin, speeding up her pulse and sending her thoughts into overdrive. He was watching Alex's house, waiting for his chance to go inside.

Alex can't be alone.

She put the car into drive and peeled out of the parking lot, wishing for the first time in her life that she had a damn cell phone so she could tell Alex to watch his back until she got to him.

ANSWER THE DOOR. PLEASE ANSWER the door.

She hit the doorbell for the third time, following up with a rapid, impatient knock. She'd already tried turning the knob, but Alex had locked himself inside. At least, that was what she assumed because his truck sat in the driveway.

When the door still didn't open, Sophie half wished she could just turn around and go back to her apartment and her life, and forget she'd ever met the man. As much as she wanted him to be home and safe, the thought of actually confronting him again after the conversation they'd had that morning made her want to curl up in a ball on his balcony and whimper. She made herself hit the bell again, just to negate the wimpy turn her thoughts had taken.

So he'd kissed her. Big deal. All she'd had to say was, "That was great, but no thank you," and they could have moved on. But noooo. Instead, she had to go all Mexican soap opera on him, ranting about how he was a player, how he didn't take her seriously, how she'd had some psychic vibe that warned her off about his superficial ways.

And the terrible thing was now she wasn't sure whether it an actual, honest-to-goodness vibe or just her own self-doubt talking. He'd been an enormous comfort to her, even leaving his ill mother's side to make sure she was okay. And she'd paid him back by acting like a first-class drama queen with an insecurity problem.

She walked along the balcony to the nearest window. Setting the stack of printouts she carried on the ground, she cupped her hands around her eyes to block out the glare and peered inside. Half expecting to see him sitting in that ugly chair of his, she wasn't prepared for the pang of worry that hit her when she saw that the room was empty.

The fact of the matter was she was terrified of Alex, of everything her instincts told her about him, of everything he made her feel. For one thing, he was ridiculously good-looking, and she…wasn't. Which, when you took her non-size-two self-doubt out of the equation, still added up to the fact that an average woman would have a hard time competing with the Amandas of the world.

Not that it stopped her from wanting to try.

She'd had dates and even long-term boyfriends before, of course, but they'd always been manageable, orderly little affairs. They had to be—she'd learned early on to always prepare herself in case the man in her life got spooked by her strange semi-psychic ability rearing its head one too many times. But what she felt now, for a man she barely knew, seemed more intense than all of the guys in her past put together. And there was no preparing herself—the thought of watching Alex grow increasingly uncomfortable with her and her unpredictable conversational turns made her want to run away herself before he could.

"But your whole relationship started with a premonition," she said into the glass. "It's not like he doesn't expect that from you."

"Who doesn't expect what from you?" a familiar voice asked.

Of course he was standing behind her. Because that was the way her life worked. Relief mixed with mortification as Sophie dropped her hands and slowly turned around. "Hey." She gave him a lame little wave.

He arched an eyebrow—something she'd never been able to do, even when she'd practiced in a mirror—but he didn't say anything else. He didn't have to—his whole demeanor suggested she was the equivalent of chewed-up gum stuck to the bottom of his hiking boot. Dropping her gaze to the pile of paper on the ground near her boots, she knew she had to just push everything she felt, including her embarrassment, aside. The information on those printouts was bigger than her argument with Alex, bigger than their morning drama and bigger than Amanda's "fat girlfriend" comment. She would be running away from this man who made her feel way too much as fast as her squashy thighs would carry her, otherwise.

"Look." Pausing to chew on her lower lip, she picked up the stack and hugged it to her chest. A biting westerly wind sprang up and blew her hair in her face and threatened to topple her off his balcony entrance. "I know we had a difficult morning—"

"So you decided to start stalking me?"

"—but I have some—" She was so absorbed in trying to remember the speech she'd practiced in the car to regain his confidence, it took a moment for her to notice that he'd insulted her. "Don't flatter yourself. I have better things to do with my time." She quashed the urge to throw the stack of papers at him.

His cool expression shifted into that cocky half grin of his, but instead of radiating warmth and fun the way it usually did, his smile felt angry. "Nice comeback, Soph. Didn't think you had that in you."

She rolled her eyes. Well, he was mad, but at least he was still speaking to her, although it was hard to feel grateful for that at the moment. "I'll have you know I have a dizzying high IQ and could verbally crush you like a bug if I ever needed to."

The eyebrow shot upward once more and he moved toward her, stepping into her space so she had to look up to keep eye contact. "Oh, is that why you're running from me—I'm not smart enough for you?"

"Is that— Oh, shut up." She clutched her papers to her. "It was a bad joke. You're plenty smart, and I'm not a snob."

"Could've fooled me."

"What?"

The wind picked up again, plastering his sweat-shirt to his chest and blowing her hair in about four different directions. "You're always flirting and being charming, Alex." He pitched his voice up into a mocking falsetto, flailing his hands around in a stereotypically feminine fashion. "And you make everyone love you because you're funny and cute and the life of the party, Alex. But you're too busy partying and being a shallow creep to handle any-thing real, Alex."

Oh, God, she'd never wanted the earth to open up and swallow her more than she did at this moment. This had to be the most uncomfortable conversation she'd ever had in her life, and while she knew she had to get it back to her original purpose for coming here, she wondered if she'd be able to. Everything had gone so wrong and she didn't know how it had happened. "I never said you were a shallow creep," she said softly.

"No, you just implied it very strongly."

"I just meant that you seem to have a lot of—" one of her hands flailed in the air, as if it could capture the words she needed out of the cold winter air "—women in your life."

"You've met *one* woman." He held up an index finger and shoved it toward her angrily. "I'm sorry Amanda's crazy and rude and showed up out of the blue, but I haven't been with her in over a year."

"There's more than one." Humiliation fueled her anger and she slammed the papers she'd been carrying into a nearby deck chair, trying not to dwell too long on the fact that Alex thought she felt petty jealousy over Amanda. And when he raised his chin at her in a clear challenge, she took it without thinking. "There's the lovely and charming Amanda, of course, whom you obviously dated for her mental acuity." She ticked off a finger. "Then there's Penny, the commuter businesswoman scorned—remember the blog I found between our first and second meeting?" She ticked off a second finger, then took a deep breath, figuring she might as well go crazy and really scare him. "And then, when I first met you, the name Trina kept flashing in my head—sound familiar?"

Backing away, Alex scrubbed a hand down his face, staring at her in clear disbelief. Yep, that should kill off any last bit of misplaced attraction he had for her.

"I thought that name was a mistake then, but I'm feeling lucky today." She dropped her hands, planting them on her hips and perversely enjoying the fact that she now had the upper hand. "I say she was probably yet another ungodly beautiful ex-girlfriend who probably overlapped with Penny somewhere."

He opened his mouth to reply, then just bared his teeth and shook his head in disbelief. "You don't know what you're talking about, Sophie."

Oh, he so did not just challenge her. "I may be a

bad psychic most of the time, but when I'm right, I'm right."

His jaw worked for a moment and when he spoke again, his voice was deadly soft. "You think when I kissed you, that it wasn't real? That it didn't mean anything?"

She shrugged. "Sure it did. It meant you had an itch that needed—" The rest of her sentence died away when his face darkened, his brown eyes looking almost black in anger. He'd been inching closer to her the whole time, and she hadn't noticed until now, when he was nearly on top of her. Looking down at her, he clearly seemed to be enjoying the effect his proximity had on her, a corner of his beautiful mouth quirking upward. And then he dipped his head so his mouth brushed hers, and she forgot what she'd been saying, forgot what she'd been feeling before. Because there was just too much to feel now.

Almost of their own accord, her arms wrapped around his neck, her fingers threading through the short dark hair at the nape. She pressed her body against his, loving the feel of him and wishing there weren't so many layers of fabric between them. The winter air grew more bitterly cold by the second, but her entire body felt as if it were radiating heat. She opened her mouth and his tongue brushed hers, then he pulled back slightly, his lips teasing, nibbling gently on hers. And she clutched at him, not wanting him to stop, not ever wanting him to stop.

But he did stop. And though she couldn't help but clutch at his sweatshirt, she let him.

He rested his forehead against hers and they both stood like that for what seemed like a long time, trying to catch their breath.

"That was real," he finally said. "Just in case you were wondering."

Sure, on an empirical level, he had most definitely kissed her.

He straightened, pulling his head back to look at her more squarely, and she felt boneless at the desire she saw in his eyes. "And just for the record, it feels like a lot more than an itch."

She felt half-tempted to throw the compliment back at him, but deflected it instead. "I, uh… I have something to show you." She pulled out of his arms, ignoring the *this-isn't-over* look he gave her, and hurriedly moved to pick up the papers she'd abandoned in his deck chair. Flipping the stack around, she pushed it toward him like a shield, holding it up so he could see the letter to the editor she'd printed out from the *Rapid City Journal*. "I think I know why your father went after those men from Centrix. At least, part of it."

That got his attention. "Seriously? That bunch of papers is about Centrix and my father?"

"Yes." She pushed aside the disappointment she felt that he'd taken her bait. "I was at the library on campus, and I couldn't stop thinking about Millie." *And you.* "Which had me wondering about the murders of these board members and the attack on your mother. They all feel…related and yet unrelated. You know what I mean?"

He narrowed his eyes at her and considered that for a moment. "Not really."

She motioned with her head toward his front door. "Can I show you inside? It's freezing out here."

He shook his head, looking a little dazed and embarrassed that he hadn't invited her in before. "Sure."

"So I remembered that both you and Wilma Red Cloud had come from the Pine Woods Reservation in South Dakota." Once inside, she made a beeline for the breakfast-nook table, a strange kind of excitement at what she'd discovered taking over. "I couldn't concentrate when I was trying to study at the library today, because I kept mulling the pieces over—your family, Millie and me, Pine Woods, Centrix, your father." She spread the papers out on the tabletop before him. "So I started with Centrix and Pine Woods, and I found this."

She pulled an article featuring a wan-looking Native American boy of about ten, lying in a hospital bed, a bandanna tied around his head to hide the fact that he was completely bald. The headline read Childhood Cancer Rates Skyrocket at Pine Woods. "The year before Wilma Red Cloud was murdered, certain anonymous Pine Woods residents started accusing Centrix of burying barrels of waste from its South Dakota factory on the reservation. Illegally, of course." Tapping the photo with one finger, she glanced up at Alex, who regarded her with a thoughtful expression.

"And they thought the illegal dumping was related to the increased childhood cancer?" he asked, making the connection between the article she'd shown him and what she'd just said.

"Yes, that and birth defects, infertility, chronic and unexplained illnesses and increased cancer in adults, too." She laid out a few more articles, the headlines of which would confirm everything for him. "The federal government largely ignored the outcry. Until, from what I can tell, a very articulate and angry Pine Woods resident started writing letters to the editor. To the *Rapid City Journal*, the *Sioux Falls Argus Leader*, and even the *Washington Post* and the *New York Times*." She shuffled through the remaining stack and produced editorial pages from each of those papers. "According to one article I found, police even suspected the letter writer of breaking into the local Centrix facility and setting one of the labs on fire. Whatever he did, his words sparked some massive protests across the state, making it really hard for the government to ignore the problem."

Alex picked up the nearest article and quickly scanned it, then set it back down. "So you've tied Centrix to the reservation my family used to live on, but what does that have to do with my father?"

She pushed one of the editorial pages across the table to him. "Alex, look at the signature of the letter writer."

He pulled the page closer and she could tell by his expression exactly when he'd seen what she wanted him to see.

Crow Carrier.

"If your father did murder Wilma Red Cloud, his timing couldn't have been better. By killing the first female leader of the Oglala Sioux, he'd brought the national spotlight to Pine Woods, and consequently, to Centrix's dirty dealings there. Lakota activists gained a national platform through his actions, and they used it well."

Scanning the articles on the table, Alex pulled one out of the stack and tapped the paper with the back of his hand. "Centrix ended up paying restitution to the reservation leaders and families."

Sophie nodded. "They would have needed to get away from the bad publicity."

The look he gave her then was one of undisguised admiration, and though it made her slightly uncomfortable, she reveled in it, too. "How did you find all of this?" he asked.

"Magic?"

The corners of his mouth quirked upward and she couldn't help but feel relieved that an unspoken peace had settled between them. "Right."

"Actually, LexisNexis."

The half smile still in place, he planted his palms on the table and leaned toward her. "Thank you."

"Sure." She expected he would gather up the articles to read more closely, or maybe walk to the door to show her out, but he did neither. Instead, he just looked at her, really looked at her. And all she could do was look back.

Oh, my, he was beautiful.

His eyelids lowered and a slow, private smile spread across his face. He bit his lower lip, still grinning at her, and the effect made her feel as though he were the psychic one and could read her like a book. If there hadn't been a table between them, she knew he would have kissed her again. And the impulse to grab him by his sweatshirt and drag him across the table to her had her backing away and blinking rapidly in an effort to shake off her desire-fueled stupor. She had to get her head back on straight or she'd slide into a pathetic little puddle at his feet, and then —

Then she'd really be in trouble.

"Speaking of interviews…" Ducking her head, she shuffled through the remaining sheaf of papers she still held. "I think you need to talk to Rebecca Red Cloud. She's the current tribal-council president on Pine Woods." Once she found what she was searching for, she handed him a sheet of paper with a phone number on it. "She's also Wilma Red Cloud's younger sister."

ALEX MUST'VE STARED at the phone in his bedroom for at least fifteen minutes before he got up the guts to pick it up and even think about dialing the number. And then he slammed it right back down again, thinking immediately of about a thousand things he'd rather be doing than chasing down his possibly murderous father's past.

Starting with picking Sophie up off the living-room chair where he'd left her, carrying her into his bedroom and doing his damn best to make her forget all of her reservations about wanting him. Because he wanted her. More than he'd ever wanted anyone in his life.

Usually, whenever he'd felt something similar to this, he'd just charm the woman into bed and, as Sophie had so eloquently put it, scratch that particular itch. But he'd meant it when he'd said that Sophie wasn't an itch. She'd freaked him the hell out at first, of course, but once he'd started to believe in her sometimes-psychic abilities, he'd realized he actually liked her. She was sweet; she made him laugh; and she gave him more evidence every time they met that she was a good person.

He also wanted her with a desire that blindsided him.

But she seemed so frightened, so protective of herself, that he knew he couldn't treat her like an oversexed flight attendant who felt like scratching her own itch on the handful of dates a year she flew into town. Sophie wasn't the kind of woman you could love and leave. She wanted something *real*.

Which normally would have sent him running for the hills, but...

Not today.

Maybe this was real. Maybe he was ready.

Sitting down heavily on the edge of his king-size bed, he clutched the cordless phone receiver in one hand, running his fingers through his hair with the other. Maybe he was just completely jacked up by the fact that he couldn't wrap her around his little finger with a smile and a compliment, and he craved the challenge. Deep down, maybe he was too shallow for her, and he didn't want to admit it before he got what he wanted.

He looked down at the phone. Maybe he needed to stop thinking with what was in his pants, formidable though it was, and think about stopping the person or persons who had nearly killed Sophie, and then he could figure out the rest.

Glancing at the phone number on the sheet of paper he'd left on his nightstand, he played through in his mind what he would say—

Damn, his sheets smelled like flowers.

Pushing off the bed, he paced the room in front of the big bay windows overlooking the mountains, moonlight bouncing off their snowy caps.

Dial the phone. Dial the freaking phone.

But that presented a whole new set of problems. What the hell was he going to say to Rebecca Red Cloud? "Hello, how are you? By the way, my father murdered your sister and I think he's killing again. Can you help me?" Right, that would get him really far.

After trying out a few explanations in his head,

all of which sounded lame, he finally just punched the number in on the keypad. Being that it was Sunday night, he seriously doubted that any council member would be in the tribal office to pick up the telephone, anyway.

"Hello, this is Rebecca Red Cloud," a strong female voice answered on the second ring.

"Um, uh…yeah, uh." Alex lightly pounded his fist against his forehead. Not the most eloquent beginning to their conversation. "Ms. Red Cloud?"

"Yes?" Surprisingly, there was no hint of impatience in her tone. Yet.

"I didn't expect you to be there." *Get it together, idiot.*

He heard her laugh softly. "Would you like me to hang up and let the machine get your call next time?"

"No! No, that's okay." Still pacing, he mentally cursed himself for not thinking more about what he would say. "My name is Alex."

"Alex who?"

She *would* ask that. "Uh, Brennan." At the last second, he decided that honesty might not be the best policy and figured it was safe to lie about his identity, since his number was unlisted and his name wouldn't display on a caller ID screen. "I'm a…private investigator looking into the Centrix Corporation. I hoped to talk to you about their dealings on the reservation." Well, he was investigating, and it was for private purposes. He figured it wasn't that much of a stretch of the truth. "I was wondering if you would be willing to answer some questions." He pitched his voice a little deeper than usual in an attempt to sound confident and professional. Maybe she'd forget about his blithering at the beginning of the call.

She inhaled slowly, then blew out a noisy breath. "I'm not sure what I would have to tell you. Their factory near Pine Woods has been closed for some time now."

"No, I'm looking into their actions twenty-some years ago," he said. "I was reading some old letters by someone who called himself 'Crow Carrier.' Do you—"

"No." A sharp click sounded in his ear and then the dial tone followed.

He glared at the phone and pushed the hang-up button. Either he'd touched a nerve or someone really hated crows.

He moved his thumb toward the redial button, then stopped, letting it hover over the receiver.

She might not be willing to talk to him.

Which meant he'd be at a dead end.

Which would put his mother and possibly Sophie in even greater danger because if he couldn't figure out what Jack Runningwater's motives were, he wouldn't be able to predict his next move. And predicting his next move was the only thing that would save any of them.

Your father didn't kill Wilma Red Cloud.

His mother's words chose that moment to come

back to him, but he couldn't even deal with that possibility. Nothing else made sense.

And that was why he needed to talk to Rebecca. He pressed the redial button once more.

"This is Rebecca Red Cloud." Her voice sounded wary, making him doubly glad she had answered rather than taking the phone off the hook.

"Yes, Ms. Red Cloud. This is Alex Brennan again. It's really important that I speak to you." When only silence greeted him, he pushed further. "People are being murdered."

"I won't talk to you on the phone," she replied, her words clipped with an angry edge.

"But I—"

"I said I won't talk to you *on the phone*," she interrupted, putting special emphasis on the last three words. "A smart P.I. like you ought to be able to figure out what to do next…Mr. Brennan." The way she spat out his name panicked him slightly. She sounded as if the fake name wasn't fooling her. "Good night."

She hung up on him once more and this time he didn't call her back, choosing instead to go into the living room where Sophie sat. When he entered the room, she rose out of the recliner to greet him, using the remote to click off the television. "What happened? What did she say?"

He glanced at his computer, still sitting on the table. "I think I'm going to South Dakota."

"I'm going with you. You're going to need me," she replied.

Chapter Nine

Alex watched the scenery of his childhood roll by as they drove toward Pine Woods, grateful that Sophie somehow sensed that he needed quiet, that he needed as much space as she could give him inside the small confines of a rental car. He'd thought Port Renegade's weather was cold, but the South Dakota winter felt brutal, and he'd cranked the little Honda's heater up full blast.

They'd been driving for about an hour after having landed in Rapid City, heading for the small, Lakota-owned hotel near the tribal offices where they planned to stay. So far, they'd been driving through wide-open grassy plains, whose flat brown surfaces stretched out as far as the eye could see in every direction in stark contrast to the rich, perpetual green of Port Renegade and pretty much all of Washington state. As they'd gotten closer to the reservation's eastern border, the terrain had gradually shifted to rolling, pine-covered hills and ridges, brown mixing with green and dotted with white patches of snow. And he'd started to remember.

The smell of burning sage and sweetgrass. The music of his father's drum, beating in time with his six-year-old heart. The sound of the buffalo pounding across the grasslands.

It all came back, things, sensations, sounds he hadn't thought about in years. He'd long ago shoved his father out of his memory and Pine Woods along with him, choosing only to remember the house in Port Renegade and the sound of his mother's voice.

He'd always felt like an imposter, pretending to be Native American when he'd assimilated into the mostly Caucasian population of his Port Renegade school and had no idea what it meant to be Lakota. But now, here, he felt as if…

As if he'd come home. As if the music of his father's last name was something to be proud of, was a name that belonged to him, instead of the vague, shadowy pseudonym his mother had imposed on them both.

And he felt other things, too. His father had given him his first basketball. He'd been the one who'd taught him to play, though Alex hadn't chosen to remember, until now.

Your ancestors were crow carriers, the strongest and most successful warriors. And you honor them with that spaghetti-armed free throw?

He'd had a sarcastic yet kind sense of humor, and

a wide smile that rarely left his face. He'd passed the curve of his nose and the tall basketball-player build down to his son. He'd passed on other things, too.

As the scenery blurred and changed during the drive with Sophie, Alex remembered traveling with his father to the edges of the reservation, to the Stronghold, where the 1890s ghost dances had been held, and to Wounded Knee, where one of the nation's worst acts of genocide against the Lakota had been committed. He'd taken him fossil hunting amid the eroded spires and buttes of the Badlands on the northern border of the reservation. Each time they'd gone, Jack had told his son to always hold on to his identity, to be proud of it.

But how could I be proud after what they said you did?

As the memories he'd pushed down and ignored for so long came rushing back, they made him confront the idea that maybe his mother had been telling the truth, that maybe his father's guilt— which he'd taken as gospel for so long—wasn't a given. Hell, even the judicial system technically considered Jack Runningwater innocent until he'd been put on trial. Aaron had told him the ritualistic murders of the Centrix board members didn't quite fit with the attack in Sophie's apartment complex or on his mother because the methods of attack were too dissimilar. And none of it fit with the man Alex thought he remembered.

And one memory especially seemed jarring given current events—the one of his father placing something silver in Alex's hands, something his piecemeal memory had turned into a badge of some sort.

Badge or not, after years of dismissing his father as a "no-good drunk," Alex was forced by the land and sky of his birthplace and the fragments of memory they held to abandon that cliché for what was real. And what was real was that Jack Runningwater had loved his family. He'd loved his son.

If he wasn't a killer twenty years ago, that doesn't mean years of being on the run haven't turned him into one.

Emotions he'd thought long buried rose up like bile and he had to fight to keep from pulling over to the side of the long, muddy road and screaming himself hoarse.

What made you leave us, Dad? What the hell told you that leaving your wife and your son behind forever was a good idea?

Something in his face must've tipped Sophie off to the dark turn his thoughts had taken because after miles of leaving him alone with his thoughts, she finally reached out to him, brushing her fingers lightly down his arm. "Alex? Are you all right?"

"Fine." But he wasn't fine, not even in the slightest. Everything he'd grown up believing, everything his mother had allowed him to think was true, had turned out to be just the lies a six-year-old boy had told himself to cope with having his life turned inside out.

"Of course you're not fine. I wouldn't be," she murmured, glancing out the windshield again at the passing scenery before turning to him once more. "Do you remember any of it?"

He remembered too much, and he didn't know how he was going to hide his relationship to this area and to the undoubtedly infamous Runningwaters once he met Rebecca Red Cloud. Glancing in the rearview mirror at his dark hair and tanned skin, he wanted to kick himself for telling the tribal president his last name was Brennan. He looked about as Irish as a tepee.

"I'm sorry, I shouldn't have asked." She patted his arm and then put her hand in her lap. He missed her touch once it was gone. "You have a lot to process right now, I'm sure. I'll just shut up now…."

"It's okay," he told her, and he meant it. Reaching out, he grabbed her hand and squeezed it, taking more than a little comfort from the feel of her slender, graceful fingers laced through his own. Maybe touching her wasn't the best idea he'd had all week, given her reaction to it the day before. But he needed to ground himself somehow, and he couldn't help it. He needed her, and he was grateful that she didn't pull away. He turned away from her slightly, glancing into the side-view mirror at the stretch of road they'd just traveled. "I'm glad you're here."

With her free hand, she ran a finger along his forearm, oblivious to the power she had. One small touch like that and she could make him forget his own name. "So am I," she said softly. "I would've hated for you to be alone here."

They'd agreed back at the airport to go right to the tribal offices, so they'd have the best chance of catching Rebecca Red Cloud today. The digital clock on the dashboard read ten minutes after four when they pulled up to their destination, which was located in a small reservation town called Kyle. The office building, a lodge-like structure made of brick and pine, sat directly in front of an elementary school. Both were surrounded by a few scattered stores and several homes that ranged from medium-sized to small and broken down, nestled in between the pine trees that had given the reservation its name. He'd heard a lot about the poverty in parts of Pine Woods, but he wasn't surprised or horrified by the more ramshackle dwellings he'd seen. To him, they belonged, like something he'd seen every day and had grown used to. It didn't mean he wouldn't change it if he could, but they felt familiar to him in ways that even parts of Port Renegade would never be.

"Do you want me to go in with you?" Sophie asked. Her reddish-brown curls cascaded down her shoulders today, the first time he'd ever seen them not partially or fully pulled up and back out of her face. "I mean, I'm not Lakota, so maybe I shouldn't be—"

"I want you to." He didn't make a move to get

out of the car. "You know, in some ways, I don't feel any more Lakota than you do." The thought left behind a bitter taste.

She pulled a lock of her hair across her chin, fingering the ends and regarding him with a thoughtful expression on her face, her other hand tightening its grip on his. "But of course you are."

"You know, he stole that from me." He knew he didn't have to explain to Sophie who he was talking about. "After my mother and I left here, it was like all of this just got wiped off the planet as far as we were concerned." He propped his wrists on top of the steering wheel, still unable to take his eyes off the door. "When we were driving, it all seemed so familiar, but now that we're going to talk to someone, I feel about as Indian as the Cleveland baseball team's mascot." He half wondered if someone was going to come outside and chase him off the reservation as an imposter.

"Ouch." Sophie watched the door with him, although he doubted her thoughts were as dumb as his own. "You know, it's not too late to stay here awhile, or come back later and find…" She let the sentence trail off.

"What, my roots?" He gave a short bark of a laugh that sounded bitter even to his own ears. "My roots start with a murderer. After that, I don't think I want to know any more."

"But you have to find out more." She pivoted in her seat, pulling her hand out of his and fixing him with a look that seemed to indicate she'd shove him out the car door if she had to. "Otherwise, we wasted a lot of money and time coming to South Dakota for lunch."

He sighed. "Right." Before he could chicken out and drive back to Rapid City, he pushed the car door open and set his feet on Pine Woods land for the first time in twenty years. He walked into the building, Sophie falling quietly into step beside him, and was almost surprised when no one challenged his right to be inside. He asked a woman working in the reception area where he could find the tribal president, and to his surprise, she simply got up and showed him to an office at the far end of the building.

He didn't remember her when he first saw her, but somewhere deep down, he knew he probably should have. Rebecca Red Cloud looked to be in her fifties, like his mother, with a slightly chubby figure she'd shoved into a pair of black pants and a bright blue button-down shirt. He barely noticed the rest of her, focusing instead on the straight sheet of straw-colored hair that fell over one shoulder. Her brow furrowed as she assessed him with a steely, confident look, and a word came to him suddenly, floating in the air between them.

Hinziwin.

The long-forgotten word meant *yellow hair*, and he knew, somehow, that that was her name in Lakota. And though the recessive genes that had given her that blond hair might have made her look less Sioux to some, it didn't make her an outsider here. Everything about her, from the snapping blue fire in her eyes to the calm authority of her presence told him she was a leader. She was the tribal president.

"Ms. Red Cloud?" She hesitated and he wondered if she was going to throw him out of her office before he'd had a chance to tell her who he was. But instead, she stepped forward to shake his hand, then Sophie's.

"Rebecca," she responded. "I'm impressed—the blond hair usually fools people into thinking I couldn't possibly be Sioux." Her handshake was firm without trying to prove something by smashing his fingers, like those of some people in powerful positions. "And you must be Alex…Brennan, was it?"

Out of the corner of his eye he saw Sophie swivel her head toward him, her mouth hanging open in surprise. Keeping his gaze on Rebecca, he aimed his foot somewhere in the vicinity of Sophie's black boot, managing to connect with its clunky heel. Sophie snapped her jaw shut.

Rebecca didn't smile at him, nor did she offer him a seat, and the challenge in her expression gave him the distinct feeling that his dropping in wasn't the best thing that had happened to her all week.

"I hope we're not intruding." He gave her his most charming smile, hoping to encourage her to relax a little. As the president of the Oglala, she probably had plenty of things to keep her busy besides some prodigal son returned to pump her for information, and he figured if he didn't get into her good graces as soon as possible, she might just clam up and throw him out before he could get anything useful out of her. And as Sophie had said, that was what they'd come for. "We could come back later—"

"No, please." She didn't return his forced cheerfulness, though she did finally gesture in invitation toward two leather-and-wood chairs in front of her desk, taking her own place behind it. "So, Irish…" Her tone indicated more than a little skepticism, and Alex had to resist the urge to squirm in his seat like a fourth grader caught talking in class.

She propped her chin on her palm, studying him as if he were a virus trapped under a microscope and she were the scientist about to eradicate him. Then, suddenly, unexpectedly, her face softened. "You want to know about the Crow Carrier?" At his nod, her eyes flicked toward the doorway. "No one's asked about him for a long time."

She absentmindedly picked a piece of lint off her desk blotter, and just when he thought she might remain lost in her memories for the rest of the afternoon, Rebecca rose from her chair, propping her hands on top of her desk. "Not here." Grabbing her black wool overcoat off a nearby coat tree, she veered around the desk and toward the door. "I need to show you something first."

Without turning around once to make sure they

were following, Rebecca led them to her car—a respectable-looking light-gold four-door with a spotless interior. He got in the front seat, Sophie in the back shooting him well-that-was-easy looks, and then Rebecca started driving.

It was easy. Too easy.

The whole journey took about forty-five minutes, and Rebecca didn't say a word the entire time. He'd been tempted to start up a conversation, but the fear that she'd clam up and challenge his right to come on her turf demanding information made him hold his tongue. Sure, as a full-blooded Oglala Lakota, he had every right to be on Pine Woods. He could build a house there and get a job as a local tour guide if he wanted. But as the son of the man who very well may have murdered her sister? He had no right to ask her for anything, and she'd undoubtedly tell him to go to hell if she knew who he was. So he'd let her reveal what she wanted to reveal on her own timetable, in her own fashion.

When she finally shut off the engine, the car sat in the parking lot of a school. A very old, very abandoned school situated on the grassy plain leading up to the eroded spires and flattened hills that signified the beginning of South Dakota's famous Badlands. Even covered with a patchwork of snow, the reds, golds and browns of the clay and sediment formations burst through in colorful splendor.

"I could tell you about this place, but I thought you should see it," Rebecca said, seemingly unable to take her eyes off the scene in front of her as she got out of the car.

Sophie and Alex followed her, the cold air hitting them like a wall of ice water when they stepped out of the car's warm interior. He scanned the building ahead, curious about what significance something so long ago abandoned could hold for them. The formerly cream-colored paint on the outside of the school grew darker along the roof and window lines, where chalky brown dust had collected, driven into every crevice by the wind. Most of the windows were devoid of glass, except for a few broken shards that remained on the edges. The winter sun couldn't penetrate the blackness inside, so every window looked like a dark, open mouth, the few shards of broken glass that still clung to some of the chipped panes like haphazard teeth furthering that illusion. Thick chains wrapped around the handles of the double doors, secured tightly with a large padlock. Completing the whole cheery scene was a dilapidated swing set that sat crookedly in what had been the school's play yard, the swings moving back and forth on the wind, squeaking painfully on chains rusty from disuse.

"My nieces attended this school, Rachel and Christina." Rebecca's slim black boots crunched across a patch of dirty snow. She stopped talking when the brutal South Dakota wind picked up, tearing at their jackets and whipping her pale hair across her face. They steeled themselves against it like three redwoods, huddling into their heavy coats until it finally died down and they could hear each other once more. It obviously hadn't snowed in several days, but the air felt heavy and the gray, pregnant clouds above looked as if they could let several inches loose at any minute.

"We were stunned when the doctor told us Christina had leukemia." Rebecca chewed lightly on her lower lip. "She was eight."

Sophie gasped softly. Alex almost didn't want to hear the rest of the story, knowing what that little girl and her family had suffered, knowing that his father may have compounded it.

"And then more children who attended this school came down with cancer—so many, it seemed like more than just a coincidence." Though the bitter cold compelled Alex to shift in place to keep his blood circulating and Sophie's fair skin had gained a slight blue tinge, Rebecca seemed oblivious to the frigid air. Apparently, Alex had chosen to block out the memory of midwestern winters.

"We read a little about this. What happened to the kids, Rebecca?" Sophie asked through chattering teeth. She wore an off-white fitted ski jacket and had tucked her hair into a soft blue winter hat, but she shivered beside him as if she'd soaked her clothes in ice water before coming outside.

"More people in this area started getting sick. Babies were born with strange abnormalities and genetic disorders. And then one day, right over there—" she pointed to an area a few feet beyond the swing set "—one of the teachers noticed the edge of a barrel poking out of the ground." She started walking in that direction, and they followed. "Toxic waste. It was illegal. And it was killing us."

Even though the school had been abandoned long ago, it wasn't hard to picture children chattering excitedly to each other in the yard, playing on the swing set or throwing balls to each other in the field beyond. The thought that they'd been playing on poisoned land, touching it, breathing its dust, sickened him. Sophie wrapped her arm through his, hugging it to her side, and he knew she understood what he felt.

"More barrels erupted in the play yard," Rebecca continued. "More children got sick. My niece survived her cancer, but so many didn't."

"We read that the waste dumping was tied to the Centrix Corporation," Alex said.

She pointed to the north, where the flat, dusty land rose up into the rugged buttes and peaks of the Badlands. "A few miles in that direction, just across the reservation borders, there's a Centrix chemical plant. It was, of course, the first place we looked, but it wasn't on our land, so without the U.S. government behind us…" Dropping her hand, Rebecca curled her lip in disgust. "It was clear that someone had been dumping their toxic chemicals on our land for years. And they didn't say anything, even when we started building a school and homes here."

"Did you have proof, when you went to the government?" Sophie asked, undoubtedly remembering the articles she'd found.

Rebecca turned toward Sophie. "Well, the barrels were unmarked, and no one could find records of the dumping. But the next nearest facility generating this kind of waste was over a hundred miles from Rapid City, near Pierre. It seemed obvious to us that Centrix was the place to start looking."

Then she leveled her icy blue gaze at him. "But you wanted to know about the Crow Carrier."

With that, she turned and started walking through the play yard, Sophie and Alex following behind her once more. When she'd gotten a few yards beyond the school, so the car was no longer visible, they were in full view of the few ramshackle homes that had also been abandoned in the area.

"What I'm about to tell you is very dangerous information. It's not too late to walk away."

"We're already in the middle of this," he responded, trying to keep the impatience he felt out of his voice. "Anything you have to say couldn't get us into any more trouble."

With a lift of her eyebrows, she shoved her hands in the pockets of her long wool coat, and he couldn't help but think that she could see right through him, that she knew exactly why he wasn't about to walk away. "Not many people know that the Crow Carrier was a man named Jack Runningwater."

Alex steeled himself to keep from flinching at

the sound of his father's name. "The man who murdered your sister," he said instead.

The wind flared up again, lifting her hair so it looked like a thousand yellow snakes dancing around her head. Then, the wind changed direction, hitting him right in the face and chilling him to the bone just as she turned toward him. He felt Sophie's arms curl protectively around his elbow as she plastered herself to his side, and he'd never been more grateful for her presence.

"And your father," Rebecca said quietly.

Chapter Ten

The soft-spoken phrase slammed into Alex like a freight train—and he couldn't have been more shocked if he had actually been run over by one.

So she knew. Despite the clever idea to use an Irish name to explain his black hair and dark features. And she'd taken him and Sophie to a deserted location, where no one would ever know if she shot them both in revenge for her sister and buried the bodies under the floorboards of the contaminated school. He instinctively tried to shield Sophie by putting himself between her and Rebecca.

But then Rebecca's face softened. "Do you remember him at all?" she asked. "Did Anna keep any pictures of him?"

By *him*, she had to mean Jack Runningwater. "No." He'd looked for old photos, in storage closets and bureaus throughout their home when he was a child. But all of the albums his mother had kept had only photos of the two of them, as if his father had never existed.

Stepping forward to close the space between them, Rebecca scanned his face, a faraway expression on her own. "You're the spitting image of him," she said. "If you grew your hair long, you'd look just like he did last time I saw him."

He had no response to that, so he kept silent. He couldn't help but feel a peculiar sort of pride at the supposed resemblance, not untouched by a vague longing he'd thought he'd overcome ages ago. But until he could prove otherwise, being Jack Runningwater's son still seemed nothing to be proud of. "That can't be easy for you, seeing as he—"

"I never quite believed Jack killed my sister."

"You—" Alex felt his whole body go slack with surprise as his mother's words came back to him. *Jack didn't kill her. He just took the fall for it.*

She motioned with her head back toward the parking lot. "Let's go back to the car. There's much you need to know, and there are eyes and ears all around this place, even when you can't see them."

He'd spent so long identifying his father as a murderer that he'd been afraid to fully believe the information Anna Gray had given him. But now Rebecca, the sister of the woman his father had supposedly murdered, the one person who probably had every right to believe conventional wisdom about the death of Wilma Red Cloud, said the same thing. And with that one sentence, he started to truly wonder whether everything he'd ever known about his family had been a lie.

Once they'd resumed their places inside the vehicle, Rebecca turned over the ignition and continued. "I brought you here so you could see with your own eyes what they did, what they're capable of." She put the car in reverse and backed away from the school, then changed gears and drove off, speeding down the snow-lined prairie road and leaving the decaying building and its poisoned grounds behind. "Some people thought Jack was a spy for Centrix, and that he murdered my sister when she got too close to learning the truth about what they'd done."

Sophie leaned forward in the back seat, getting as close to the conversation as her seat belt would allow. "But he wasn't? He was the one writing the letters to the newspapers, to focus national attention on what was going on."

Rebecca nodded. "He was a tribal policeman. Wilma told me that he was working on something to do with Centrix, something big. But I never found out what it was. She was killed, and Jack went underground. As far as I know, none of us ever saw him again." She glanced at Alex. "Or you and your mother."

"She was ashamed," Alex murmured, watching the brown grass of the plains go by, dotted with snow. The broad cumulus clouds had grown heavier and darker while they'd been gone, stretching across the sky and covering every last swatch of blue, and he knew it meant the weather would take a turn for the worse that night. He hoped they'd still be able to catch their flight the next day. "She told me she couldn't face anyone who lived here after what my father did, especially your family."

Rebecca clicked her tongue against her teeth, shaking her head as she focused on the stretch of road in front of her. "That's one thing I could never figure out. Anna defended Jack fiercely right after Wilma died. And then, she suddenly grew quiet and slipped away in the middle of the night like a field mouse." She slanted a glance at him. "Anna Runningwater was no field mouse."

"You said he was trying to get the nation to see what was going on at Pine Woods," Alex said, weighing his words carefully. "Wilma's death accomplished that."

Rebecca smiled vaguely, knowing exactly where he was going. "That company killed our children, and they didn't make it right until every newspaper in the nation called them on their actions. I don't doubt for a minute that they could have killed my sister. And I've never believed that Jack would do that."

"Not even to draw attention to the cause?" Sophie asked from the back seat. "If he blew up a lab, it sounds like he was getting desperate."

"I've gone back and forth on Jack's guilt or innocence. Wilma was my sister, and for the longest time, I had to blame someone," she said, keeping her eyes on the road. "But blame lies with that corporation. They proved when they poisoned our land that our lives don't matter to them. But they mattered to Jack. Everything he did was to avenge our people, not kill them. Not even one of them for the whole."

She sounded so sure, defending his father when even his own mother had remained silent for so long.

The rest of the drive went by quickly. Rebecca asked about Anna, and he told her what had happened to his mother, filling her in on the threats and violence that had occurred in the last few days. She talked about Pine Woods and the plans she had as tribal president, as well as about what it had been like shortly after he and his mother had left. Too soon, they pulled back into the council office parking lot.

Once Sophie had said her goodbyes and had gotten into the passenger side of their rental car, Rebecca surprised him by leaning forward and embracing him. "I remember you, when you were small, toddling along behind your mother or with your father." She pulled away quickly and for a moment her regal bearing had been replaced by an almost maternal one. "When this is all over, you should come back."

Back. He wanted to, but for some reason, the thought of being treated as an outsider after so many years living away from the reservation made him hesitate. "Does everyone have the same view of my father as you do?"

"Does it matter? You're not your father. But you are Lakota." Her mouth turned up in a wry smile. "You have to claim your roots and make your own way, Alex. They won't come to you."

He smiled back at her and walked around to the driver's side of the car. But before she'd even turned to reenter her office building, he stopped her with a question. "If my father didn't kill Wilma, do you think he's still alive?" As soon as it was out of his mouth, he felt ridiculous. She wouldn't have any more of an idea than he would.

But Rebecca appeared thoughtful, as if she actually considered his question a sane one. "She can tell you." She gestured to where Sophie sat inside the car, fiddling with the radio. "She sees with…we call it *chante ista*, the single eye of the heart." She curled her hand up just beneath her collarbone, over her own heart. "I don't have that ability, but I've seen enough people who do to know. Stay close to her. She's going to be very important to you before this is all over."

AFTER HAVING DINNER in the hotel restaurant, Sophie fired up her battered laptop while Alex called the hospital for the third time that day to check on his mother, then jumped in the shower. She tried to finish up her term paper, hoping to e-mail it to her professor before midnight so she'd at least meet the deadline, even though she'd missed class today. She'd brought a few of the more useful books and articles with her, and they lay scattered across the beige-and-red flowered bedspread on which she sat, within easy reach.

But try as she might to surround herself with things of an academic nature, she couldn't focus to save her life. For one thing, she'd been forced to ask Alex if he'd mind sharing a room to keep expenses down, given her limited earning power as a grad student—and boy, had the suggestive comments flown fast and furious after that one. So here they were, confined together in a small room dominated by a soft, rather gigantic bed. As if that weren't distraction enough, the sound of the water running reminded her that on the other side of that bathroom door, Alex was standing in the shower. Naked. And wet. And really, really out of her league.

Or was he? Her friends always told her not to sell herself short. She studied her reflection in the large mirror opposite the bed, reaching up to finger-comb a few stray locks of hair into place. She may not have model-perfect looks, but she wasn't bad. Even though she hovered between a not-so-tiny size twelve and fourteen, the extra weight distributed itself to her best advantage—generally going to her chest and hips instead of her stomach, so she had an hourglass shape no matter how many extra lattes she consumed. She'd always liked her hair. The endless freckles and pale skin that refused to tan, not so much, but they weren't awful. And she was pretty nice and fairly intelligent, if she did say so herself. All in all, not a bad catch.

So why did she feel so sure Alex Gray was going to break her heart?

Most of the men in her past had gotten spooked by her random psychic visions, which seemed to increase in frequency and freakiness the more involved she got with someone—all the better to ultimately chase him away. But Alex seemed to be on his way to actually accepting that part of her, and because of the situation with his father, seemed even to want her to tap into it more.

His flirtatious nature worried her a little—it was hard to tell when his compliments were genuine and when he was just teasing. But even the worst players eventually settled down when they found the right person.

So what was her problem?

The bathroom door opened, and when she saw Alex standing there in a pair of long blue basketball shorts and nothing else, droplets of water clinging to the golden skin of his taut, muscular, perfect chest, she knew exactly what a good part of her problem was.

She'd never wanted a man this much in her life. And the thought of having him and losing him scared her to pieces.

Wrapping one of the hotel's fluffy white towels around his neck, he sauntered over to the second, unoccupied bed, oblivious to the fact that she felt like spontaneously combusting.

"How's the paper going?" he asked, lowering himself to the mattress.

It wasn't, but she couldn't admit that to him. "Great. I just have to figure out my concluding paragraphs, and it'll be out of my hair." That, at least, was true, since she'd finished up most of it at the library the day before.

Stretching his legs across the bed, he settled back into the pillows, tugging at the ends of the towel so it hugged his neck. "So, a Ph.D. in art history, huh?"

"Yep." She started tapping on the keys, typing out a stream-of-consciousness ending paragraph that she'd go back and fix later, like maybe after a cold shower. "I suppose you're wondering what I'm going to do with it?" Everyone wanted to know what she planned to do with a seemingly useless and expensive degree.

He shrugged. "I'm guessing you could teach, or work in a museum. I'd rather hear about the paper you're working on."

She slanted a skeptical glance at him. "No, you wouldn't."

Rolling over on his side, he propped his head up on his elbow. "Why wouldn't I? I actually used to like doing term papers in college."

Well, why not? It wasn't as if they had anything else to do, besides watch TV. "It's just a short, easy paper. I'm looking at the theme of alienation in three works by Degas, Hopper and Segal."

Pushing off the mattress, he rose and walked over to her bed, idly nudging one of her books so he could see the pages. "Give me an example."

She picked up one of the books and flipped through the pages, until she found the image she wanted. "Here, this is Hopper's *The Nighthawks*." She handed him the book. "You have two people in a bar, which is usually a very companionable place, where perfect strangers can meet and talk, spill their problems to the bartender, or whatever. But the lone customer sits there hunched over his drink, and the bartender is all the way on the other end cleaning glasses."

She moved closer to him to point at the people in Hopper's painting. "You know they're aware of each other, but they're not speaking or even looking at each other.

"Or this one." Flipping through another book until she'd found Degas's *The Glass of Absinthe,* she knew she'd crossed the line to complete nerddom, but she couldn't help herself. "These two people are sitting together in a restaurant or café, but their eyes are looking in near opposite directions. Again, it should be a companionable setting, but they're so disconnected."

He leaned toward the page, examining the painting. "I see that. Even down to their drinks— she's having absinthe, but instead of drinking with her, he decided to go for a boring, nonalcoholic cup of coffee."

She rewarded him with a grin, feeling the same kind of pleasure she always did when someone decided to indulge her. "Exactly."

"Kind of like sharing a hotel room but not jumping my bones when I'm standing here half-naked, hey, Soph?"

And just like that, the air between them grew charged. Her entire body went slack with desire, every inch of her skin zinging with the need to be touched, and she couldn't have gotten a coherent sentence out if someone had offered her free rent for a year to do it.

He winked at her, then schooled his face into a mock-serious expression. "Sorry. You were saying?"

"I—"

"Alienation? Your paper's thesis?"

Speak. You can do this. Just speak, and play it off as casually as he is. "Right." She reached up with both hands and cupped her cheeks, trying to bring herself back from the very hot, very forbidden place where her mind had gone. "The interesting thing about these pieces is that we can feel the alienation of the people in them, but for us, looking at them is a shared experience that brings us together. Unless we talk about what we see, though, we'll be as separate as the people in these works of art. Which is where the art historian comes in."

Placing the book back down on the mattress, he narrowed his eyes at her. "Are you an artist?"

She had to laugh at that one. "No. I'm awful. I could barely color in the lines as a kid."

"You're so passionate about art," he said softly. "It's the way I feel about tracking."

She quickly cleaned up the last bit of text, just

about ready to send it to her professor. "I love looking at it, and talking about it," she told him as she worked. "I love how a piece is different every time you look at it, and how it tells a million stories. I see alienation in these three pieces, but tomorrow, I could see something else entirely." Closing the document, she attached it to an e-mail and then hit Send, smiling at him. "If I could manage a gallery or work in a museum for the rest of my life, I'd be happy."

"You're really beautiful," he said.

She ducked her head. "I wish you'd stop doing that."

"Doing what?"

She reopened the document and tapped a few keys on her laptop, pretending to be absorbed in fussing with her paper again, even though it was long gone now. "Flirting."

"It's more than that, and you know it, Soph," he replied, his deep voice soft, intimate. "A woman doesn't kiss the way you do unless she's feeling something fierce."

Her fingers flew across the keyboard, her nails clicking against the letters as she banged out sentences that most likely didn't even resemble English. Against her will, her body recalled what it felt like to kiss him, and she had to stop typing to hide the sudden tremor in her hands.

"You said you thought I'd break your heart." Resting his elbows on his knees, he spoke to the far wall, not looking at her. "I can't promise I won't disappoint you somehow, but I'll tell you this, Sophie Brennan." He jammed his fingers through his hair, restless, pent-up energy making the movement jerky. "I can't sleep. I can't breathe when I'm around you, I want you so much."

That should have been enough for her, but it wasn't. Maybe his attraction had little to do with her and much to do with the fact that she hadn't immediately thrown herself at him when he'd turned on the charm. Maybe when the fire between them died down, he'd stammer a few excuses and disappear. Maybe he'd go back to his Amandas, who gave him all the physical perks of a relationship with none of the strings.

Maybe she suddenly didn't care.

Jackknifing up to a standing position, he grabbed a pillow from his bed, then strode across the room to the door to the living-room section of their suite. "There's a pull-out couch out there. I'm going to—"

He didn't get to finish his sentence. Completely beyond reason, Sophie launched herself off the bed and reached for him, turning him around by the arm to face her. Every nerve ending felt raw and exposed, and the only thing she could think about was her all-consuming need to touch him. Pressing her palms against his bare sleek chest, she shoved him up against the wall, using the towel still draped around his neck to pull him down to her.

He responded in kind, and his kiss was hard, demanding. He cupped her face with both hands, while she ran her own all over his bare chest and back, pressing her nails into his skin. She could feel how much he wanted her—he hadn't lied about that.

"Sophie," he murmured against her lips. When she didn't respond, he pulled away from her slightly, and she trailed her mouth down the sharp line of his jaw, lightly biting the tender skin on his neck. He drew in a deep, shuddering breath, and she felt an almost animalistic desire at the thought that she could affect him like that.

"Sophie." Ignoring him, she moved her mouth down his chest, still damp from his recent shower, hooking her thumb into the waistband of his shorts, fully intending to pull them off him soon. He tangled his hands into her hair. "Ah, God, Sophie," he moaned softly. She heard him breathe in, breathe out, felt his heart beating through skin and bone. "Are you sure?"

"Mmmmmmm." With a soft purr, she stopped her attentions and raised her eyes to his, her mouth feeling swollen from his kiss earlier, and every inch of her wanting more. They just looked at each other, breathing heavily, his dark eyes nearly black with desire, and then she finally remembered how to speak again. "Shut up and kiss me."

His eyelids lowered and he bit his bottom lip, giving her a slow, intimate smile that sent a shiver across her skin. Trailing his fingertips down the side of her neck, he traced a line from her collarbone to the V of her button-down shirt, pushing aside the fabric to gently caress the swell of one breast. "Then come here," he challenged. So she did.

Plunging his tongue into her mouth, he somehow managed to gracefully undo the buttons of her shirt one-handed. He pushed the material down her shoulders, and she took her hands off him just long enough to allow the shirt to slip to the floor. Cupping her rear, he pulled her against him once more, and she gasped at the erotic shock of feeling her bare skin against his.

Before she realized what he was doing, he'd lifted her up as effortlessly as if she were weightless, and she hooked her legs around his buttocks. He carried her the few steps to his bed and gently laid her on the mattress, lowering himself on top of her.

His mouth trailed against her jawline and then he nipped at her earlobe, causing an involuntary *ahh* of pleasure to escape her lips. She gripped his shoulders, digging the pads of her fingers into his skin and pushing against him until she had him on his back, straddling his waist. Her hand went to the front hook of her bra.

And then she stopped, her fingertips resting against her breastbone as the first hint of self-doubt pierced the desire-laden fog she'd been in. She glanced at the small lamp, blazing brightly on the bedside table.

When she looked down at Alex, he gave her that

same wicked smile of his. "Beautiful girl," he murmured, sitting up and gently cupping her jaw, claiming her mouth once more. When he'd stolen her breath, he pulled away, his hands slipping down to cup both of her breasts over the lace fabric. He tilted his hips, grinding against her through her jeans, and just that inadequate motion had her crying out in pleasure. Sliding his fingers over the hand she held over her bra hook, he caressed it instead of pulling it away, his message clear: it would be her decision.

She hesitated.

"Please," he breathed, touching his lips softly, teasingly against hers in swift butterfly kisses that nearly drove her mad.

Unhooking the clasp, she slipped her bra off her shoulders, feeling more vulnerable than she ever had in her life. Her jeans followed in a tricky little dance that she tried to make graceful.

He closed his eyes, inhaled sharply, and when he opened them again, his dark, intense gaze left no doubt—he still wanted her, more now than before. And she wanted him like nothing she'd ever known.

For tonight, she was beautiful.

A LOUD, SHRILL RING DISTURBED the best sleep she'd ever had in her life. With a groan, she snuggled deeper into the crook of Alex's arm, hoping the caller would realize his mistake and hang up quickly.

She ignored the third ring, and the fourth, but

when Alex stirred beside her and the hotel voice mail still didn't pick up, she figured she'd better get it. Disentangling herself from the sheets and Alex's hold on her, she reached across the bed to the nightstand and picked up the receiver, her eyes still half-closed. "'Lo?"

"Is Alex there?" a male voice asked pleasantly, as if calling at—she squinted at the bedside digital clock—3:37 a.m. were a perfectly normal thing to do.

"Yes, but he's sleeping," she answered, adding a little bite to the last word. "Who is this?"

"A friend."

The way he said it sent a chill across her bare arms and her drowsiness suddenly disappeared, the first traces of fear settling heavily on her chest. "Do you have a message for him?" she asked, taking care to keep her voice as neutral as possible. *No one knows you're here.*

"I thought I told you to stay away from him, Sophie."

Oh, God. Her eyes darted to the room's single window, barely visible in the darkness, but she'd already pulled the heavy curtains across the glass. He couldn't see in, but she couldn't see out, so for all she knew, he could be standing right outside that thin glass barrier.

He knows where you are. He's been watching you both.

She sat up quickly, clutching the phone in a

death grip. "Are you threatening me?" she whispered harshly.

The man chuckled softly in her ear. "Consider it a friendly warning."

"Warning about what?" she asked, hearing and hating the hysterical edge building in her voice. "What do you want?"

"There are eyes and ears all around this place, even when you can't see them," he said, and the words made the hair on the back of her neck prickle. Rebecca had uttered that sentence verbatim that afternoon, when she'd taken them to the deserted Pine Woods school.

"Would you tell him something for me?" the caller asked.

For a murdering stalker, he certainly was polite. "Tell him yourself."

This time, he laughed outright. "Feisty one, aren't you? Good. You'll need that." When she didn't respond, he continued. "Tell Alex to check his mail."

"What's in there?" She knew she should hang up and get them both far, far away from this place, as quickly as she could. She and Alex couldn't have been more alone than they were on this cold, remote reservation, miles away from family, friends and the Port Renegade police, who knew why they needed to be protected.

"Just tell him," he snapped. She heard a sharp click and then the dial tone sounded in her ear.

The tremor started in her hands, as she slowly

hung up the phone, and pretty soon her entire body was shaking. Alex chose that moment to roll over, flopping an arm across her midsection, sleep clearly having made him oblivious to the whole conversation. "Who was that?" he murmured drowsily, his eyes still closed.

Your father.

Chapter Eleven

Once she had woken Alex up fully and had told him what had happened, he wasted no time in getting them out of the hotel and on their way back to Rapid City. They would probably end up sitting in the airport for at least eight hours, but once they got through the metal detectors at the security checkpoints, they both knew they'd be a lot safer.

"We're going to be about eight hours early for our flight, you know," she said softly to Alex's profile, which looked fierce and angry in the dim green light from the dashboard.

"Better that than sitting in that hotel room waiting to be shot." He glanced into the rearview mirror, undoubtedly to check that they weren't being followed.

"Well, we're going back to possibly check your mail," she replied. "Maybe he won't follow and shoot us if we're on our way to pick up his letter bomb."

Alex swore viciously, and she heard the transmission grind as the car shifted into a higher gear that took them well over the posted speed limit.

It wasn't until they sped past Rapid City's outermost borders that they both relaxed a little, the dark, remote road they'd just traveled giving way to a brightly lit highway. Alex slipped the compact in between two semi trucks, and Sophie felt as if she could finally breathe again.

She wanted to reach for him, to comfort him and gain a little comfort herself, but she couldn't figure out how. So much had happened between them tonight, but now that they'd been ripped out of the dream and pulled back into the nightmare, everything they'd felt for each other seemed distant and unapproachable. She'd never know if he would have woken up and held her close, made love to her again, or if he would have pulled away, mouthing excuses and apologies. And with their lives in the balance at the moment, it probably didn't matter either way.

"I didn't mean to be flip," she said, referring to her letter-bomb comment. "What do you think could be in your mail?"

He gave her a quick, jerky shrug, glaring at the road in stony silence. Then, he suddenly started fumbling with his jacket, his hands rustling against the stiff fabric, until he'd managed to extricate something from one of its oversize front pockets. He handed it to her.

She could tell by touch that it was a thin

postcard. Reaching up, she snapped on the overhead light and squinted at the words. "It's from the post office. It says you have a certified letter."

"It's been in my pocket forever," he said. "Last time I got one of these, it was some stupid company telling me I'd won a tropical vacation as long as I sat and listened to a ninety-minute lecture about a time-share. So I ignored it." He paused and then said, "Do you think…?"

She nodded. "Yes, I think."

They drove for awhile in silence until Alex pulled the car onto the exit ramp for the airport. Reaching across the seat, he took her hand, squeezing it lightly in reassurance. His touch told her everything she needed to know, that she didn't have to be afraid of the dream.

"I'm sorry, Sophie. I wish you'd never been dragged into this," he said.

But she barely heard him, overwhelmed by the feel of his warm hand on hers and the thin postcard she also held. And something came to her in such sharp, disturbing clarity, she nearly cried out at what she suddenly realized.

Alex was going to break her heart. She'd known that all along, and she knew it still. But now, she also knew that it had nothing to do with his not feeling enough for her, with her not being enough for him.

She turned her face away from him, hoping he wouldn't notice and ask her what was the matter.

Because she couldn't ever tell him what she'd just seen, what she now knew from past experience to be an inexorable truth.

Whatever it was that threatened them would do more than just frighten them. It was a detached, calculating presence that haunted their steps, human, but with something important missing. Before this was all over, it was coming for Alex.

And it could eventually kill him.

AFTER EIGHT HOURS OF SITTING in the Rapid City airport, Alex and Sophie finally got on their flight home. He hated that their time at the hotel had been interrupted by some insane freak who may or may not be Jack Runningwater, and whenever he tried to talk to Sophie about it on the flight, she cut him off, getting up to ask for some water or telling him she wanted to sleep rather than talk.

She seemed sad whenever she looked at him, and he hated the thought that what had been the most incredible night of his life might be something she regretted.

"Sophie," he murmured into her hair as she pretended to sleep while leaning against his shoulder. "We need to talk."

She didn't respond, but the little hitch in her breathing told him she'd heard him.

Some little scrap of pride that remained told him to let it go, get away from her before she made a fool of him. But he knew even as he thought about walking away that he'd never be able to. He refused to believe that everything he felt, everything they'd done had been one-sided—until she told him point blank that she didn't feel the same.

But obviously, now was not the time, crushed together in the too-narrow seats of the airplane, with the flight attendants hovering over them and the passengers across the aisle well within earshot. If he was doomed to be humiliated, he'd rather do it in private, thank you very much.

Damn, he didn't want this to be one-sided.

When they landed in Port Renegade several hours and one connecting stop later, they discovered upon exiting the terminal that their part of Washington had experienced a storm in their absence. A thick layer of snow blanketed the landscaped areas around the parking lot, at least seven inches high, with dirt-streaked drifts deposited by snow plows that reached their knees. The air felt cool and still, without the sharp bite that indicated more precipitation was coming. Knowing the area as he did, Alex could tell that the snow probably wouldn't last more than a couple of days before melting completely. But for now, the city looked like the inside of a holiday snow globe.

When they reached his truck, he offered to drive her to her mother's or somewhere else where she'd be safe. To his surprise, she threw her arms around him, burying her face in his neck, and the sheer relief he felt at her touch nearly undid him.

"No, I'm staying with you. Every minute," she said.

So he took her to the post office to pick up the certified letter, which had the name Jim Gray and a Port Renegade P.O. box in the return address. He carefully felt the envelope, which was thin and pliable, with none of the bulges, unevenness or extra weight that bomb wires would inevitably create. He'd considered taking it to the police station so the bomb squad could examine it, but the envelope clearly held only a thin sheet of paper inside.

So he opened it, with Sophie looking on over his shoulder.

Dear Alex,

I know to you, I became an invisible man twenty years ago, one who was never there when he should have been, at least not tangibly. But I've been nearby and have watched you grow up, even when you and your mother didn't know I was there.

I wish I could tell you why I had to leave you, but a thirst for justice and a passion for revenge drove me to turn my back on the most important things in the world, and now that I am old and that passion has cooled, I find my life is one mainly of regrets. But one thing I will never regret is the action I take now to protect you.

It has taken me two decades to learn the identities of the men who poisoned your first home, who killed many of our Lakota sons and daughters and could have killed my own son, had we not acted. I have finally been able to put all the pieces in place, and gain the confidence of someone inside the organization that had much to share.

Go to that which was here before us, and find the history and the future buried there.

Please don't bring the police. My ability to keep you safe rests on my remaining invisible.
J.R.

J.R. It couldn't be.

After everything Alex and Sophie had been through, he'd been too afraid to do more than briefly entertain the idea that his father was innocent, that his father was even still alive. But the letter… He'd never felt the lack of a father more in his life than he did at that moment, and he wanted it to be true more than anything.

"Is this real?" A small frown on her face, Sophie had wrapped her arms around herself and she wouldn't look at him. "Sophie, do you know?"

He took her hand and placed the letter in it, knowing that touching it would help her get clarity. It had to give her clarity. "I believe you. I know you can tell me something."

"No." She closed her eyes and shook her head

several times. "No. There's nothing. I can't see a thing, Alex." Snatching her hand away so the slip of paper fell to the floor, she backed away from him. "I'm sorry."

He bent to retrieve it, wondering what had gotten into her. "Is there something you're not telling me? Soph, I'm a grown man—whatever it is, I can handle it."

She threw her hands up in the air, palms out and fingers splayed, clearly sending a message that she wanted him to stop bothering her. "Alex, don't pressure me. I told you I'm worthless when someone's demanding answers." She spun around and pushed through the post-office glass door, stopping when she was several feet from the entrance outside.

He followed her, scrubbing a hand down his face as anger and worry swirled together inside him. "Sophie, dammit, if you can't help me, at least talk to me. This could be *my father*." He smacked the back of his hand against the sheet of paper, nearly running into a hapless older man who was carrying a large box through the parking lot. Mumbling an apology, Alex reached out and gently steered the man out of his path as Sophie turned and waited for him to catch up. "It's all right if you can't see anything, but could you just talk to me?"

"I'm sorry." She sighed, looking as sad and lost as she had the first day he'd met her, when she'd resigned herself to being taken from the state park where he worked to the police station. It seemed like years ago, when it had only been a handful of days.

"What's up with you?" he asked her.

"What if it's a trap?"

He'd thought of that, but his gut told him that wasn't the case. Then again, his gut could be indulging in a severe case of wishful thinking. "Is it?"

She skimmed her fingers along the letter, a thin line appearing between her brows as she concentrated on it. "I don't know." She pressed her hands against her eyes, as if trying to block out the world. "God, I don't know. This is horrible."

Dropping her hands to her sides, she tugged the letter out of his grasp and skimmed it again. "Okay." Taking a deep, shaky breath, she blew it out, then continued. "Does any of this make sense to you? Like this part of going to 'that which was here before us'?"

He shrugged, searching his memory for things he'd long ago left buried.

"From an empirical, non-psychic point of view, it seems like this cryptic sentence should mean something to you." She traced a fingernail underneath the sentence she'd just quoted. "It obviously does to the letter writer."

"Go to that which was here before us and find the history and the future buried there," he murmured. Snapshots of his childhood played in his mind like a slide show. Playing basketball. Standing on the grassy plains of Wounded Knee while his father explained their history. Walking among the South Dakota evergreens.

These trees were here before us and hold histories of their own.

"He told me that every time we walked in the woods together. Every time I can remember," he said.

"Did he do anything or show you anything then?" she asked.

He nodded his head, concentrating until each piece of memory fell into place. "He always showed me the oldest and tallest tree when he did that." Putting his hand on her elbow, he steered her toward his pickup. "Come on. I think I know where he wants us to go."

SETTING THE EMPTY PACKAGE he'd carried inside the post office on a nearby ledge, Robert Felden peered through the glass doors as the red pickup pulled out of the parking lot. The two of them had disappeared for a while, but his TSA connections had managed to track them down, and he'd been there to meet them at the airport when they'd landed. Of course, they hadn't known it at the time.

Go after his family, the CEO had ordered.

He'd do better than that. He'd eliminate the son and his pretty little girlfriend, and he'd get back whatever it was that had so disturbed his boss.

He'd been so close, the son had walked right into him, and he still hadn't truly seen him. And

Robert had heard enough of the son's conversation to know that his father had finally made contact.

Go after his family.

Knock them down, one by one.

You did what you had to do.

He thought once more of the picture of his daughter in his wallet. He knew that, for her sake, he shouldn't enjoy what he did so much, that he should just stay in the cubicle and work himself to the bone instead.

But he did enjoy it.

So she'd just never have to know.

Chapter Twelve

"The only way those shoes could be worse for hiking is if you'd made them out of paper and masking tape," Alex grumbled as he pulled his truck into one of Renegade Ridge State Park's trailhead parking areas. Her black boots weren't waterproof; they had little to no traction; and the stacked heel made her balance in rugged terrain precarious at best.

Shooting him an exasperated glance, Sophie got out of the truck, and he followed. As if on cue, she took a couple of steps on the slippery pavement and then her legs started doing a little dance on a patch of ice while she windmilled her arms. Grabbing on to the open door at her side, she managed to right herself without sustaining an injury…this time.

The hike he had in mind was ridiculously easy, but her near fall on a flat surface made it difficult for him to stop dwelling on her stupid shoes. Improper footgear plus rugged terrain almost always led to accidents.

"Stop looking at me like that. I could have worn my stilettos." Managing to keep herself upright, she pulled her off-white cashmere hat out of her coat pocket and put it on, pushing a few stray locks of hair out of her face and tucking them behind her ears. "These boots will work. They do an okay job of keeping the snow out, and contrary to my little display earlier on that patch of ice, I'm used to walking in them." Tugging on her gloves, she turned and scanned their surroundings, presumably searching for the start of the trail he'd told her they would be hiking. "Besides, we don't have time to go get my tennis shoes. I'll be fine."

"Yes, you are fine." It was his stock response to that kind of remark, but there wasn't anything stock about it when it came to Sophie. Her tan corduroy pants and off-white, soft-looking sweater clung to her body, emphasized the curves he'd gotten to know well the night before, and just thinking about the night before made him want to—

Something on his face must've told her exactly in which direction his thoughts had gone because she gave him a pained look, then concentrated on zipping up her ski jacket. "Alex, don't."

"Don't what, Sophie?" He moved into her space, and her lips parted when she looked up at him. He obviously had an effect on her, so why did she insist on making this so damn difficult? "Don't remember last night? Pretend it never happened?"

She busied herself tugging on her gloves, as if

trying to get the perfect fit, but he knew she just didn't want to look at him. "Don't remember what you look like when I touch you?" he continued. "Don't remember that little sound you make when I kiss you right here?" He ran a finger down the side of her neck, just behind her ear, making her shiver.

When she didn't say anything, he decided for better or for worse, he was just going to lay it out on the line. "I don't know what you're afraid of, Soph, but you need to get over it."

Her head snapped up and she blinked at him in surprise. "I don't—"

He put his palms in the air and backed away from her, angry and hurt and desperately wanting her to see what she was doing. "You're all about excuses. You're a terrible psychic. You're too good of a psychic, so you scare people. You're bad under pressure. You don't want to get hurt. You're not pretty enough." He gave a snort of laughter that had no mirth in it. "Hell, I'm too pretty."

She made a sound that was half laugh, half stifled exclamation.

He strode back toward her, getting close, but not touching her, except to reach out and pull a lock of her hair through his fingers. "You're beautiful," he said softly. "And smart. You make me laugh, and you've got to be the nicest person I've ever met." She blinked rapidly, her dark blue eyes glistening, and he leaned forward to press a kiss on her forehead. "You're worth so much more than you give yourself credit for," he murmured against her skin. "And I'm crazy about you."

She wrapped her arms around his neck, holding on to him as if he were the only thing that kept her attached to the ground. "I saw something," she said, her voice muffled by his jacket. "Something's going to happen to—"

He pulled back abruptly, putting his hands on her arms and looking her straight in the eye so she wouldn't misunderstand his meaning. "I don't care."

"What?"

"Whatever it is, I. Don't. Care. Why can't you just stop worrying about what you're going to lose and just be with me?"

The troubled lines between her eyebrows eased, and Sophie reached up to touch his cheek with her gloved hand, the texture of the fabric as soft as fur. She inhaled deeply, squaring her shoulders. "Okay." She pushed herself on her toes, brushing her mouth lightly against his, her lips cool and soft and making him want more. "But if I'm quiet, it's just because I need to pay attention. Can you let me do that?"

He nodded, knowing they didn't have time to sort out everything that was between them. They had about an hour of daylight left to figure out where the note in his pocket would lead them. And given that Sophie had made it clear she wouldn't stand for being left behind, he didn't want to keep her out in the open any longer than he had to.

"Your shoes still suck." He grabbed her hand and led her toward the start of the trail.

A DEEP QUIET HAD DESCENDED on the woods, punctuated only by the occasional birdcall or twig snapping under the swift, light feet of a small animal. The evergreen trees towering around them all had a light layer of snow on their branches. It should have been peaceful, but it wasn't.

He still held her hand as they started down Fox Run Trail, but what she really wanted to do was wrap her arms around him and drag him back up the trail and out of the city. Out of the state, even. Anything to get away from whoever had been shadowing them for so long.

Maybe he was right, and the awful feeling she had that something bad was about to happen to him was just something she'd conjured up out of thin air to avoid risking her heart.

She couldn't tell, mainly because she hadn't been able to get a hit on anything since they'd left Pine Woods last night, as if every psychic impulse she'd ever had had just been a dream.

The too-silent woods closed in around them, tree branches heavy with snow reaching down toward them, dripping moss and tangled ferns sweeping against their arms and ankles with every step they took through the deep snow. And even though she hadn't seen or heard anyone nearby since they'd started down the trail, she couldn't shake the feeling that they were being watched. But she knew it wasn't her instinct or her psychic ability sending that message—it was just pure fear, making her afraid of everything and nothing.

Alex, of course, habitually wore Timberland shoes that could double as hiking boots in a pinch, so he easily walked through the snow, setting a brisk pace. She, on the other hand, seemed to have a gift for stepping in the deepest drifts, and she knew she slowed him down because she was constantly having to yank her foot out of the snow, only to plunge it back in well above her ankle with the next step.

Once they got farther under the tree canopy, however, the snow grew shallower, and Sophie had little trouble navigating the first half of the mile-long loop, the entirety of which had been covered with gravel to make traversing it easier. That, coupled with the fact that the trail didn't climb up the ridge but stayed rather flat, made the going easy.

As soon as they rounded the top of the loop, a gigantic evergreen came into view, its trunk appearing wider than Sophie was tall. Its bristly branches, which only grew on the top half of the tree, tapered into a neat point well over the rest of the old growth in the area.

Alex veered off the path toward the tree, taking her with him. Once again, the snow came up over her ankles, and she constantly had to weave around or push away whip-thin saplings or snarling weeds that grew in her path. When they reached the tree, she pressed a palm against the thin, furrowed bark of the ancient tree, carefully navigating between the sturdy roots that buckled and twisted before they plunged into the ground.

"It's over two thousand years old, by our estimates," Alex said as he squinted up into its highest branches. "We call it Junior."

"Wow, it's really beautiful." As soon as she'd said it, the statement felt inadequate to her. She liked trees as much as the next person, but she had to admit, she'd never given them much thought. But she didn't think anyone could help but feel a sense of awe next to something so large and…quiet. It had been wide and formidable during the Revolutionary War, had been tall and strong even when Shakespeare had written his plays. She was so busy considering the tree's history that it took a few seconds for Alex's second statement to hit her. "Why do you call it Junior?"

"He's named after a bristlecone pine in California called Methuselah that's a lot older—around four thousand eight hundred years old." Alex reached down and scooped up a handful of pine needles and snow, picking out a small twig with several still attached to show her. "This one's a western hemlock—see the flat needles?—not a bristlecone, but we call it Methuselah Jr., or just Junior."

Craning her neck, she looked once more into its tallest branches overhead, listening to the wind rustling through them. "Right. Junior. Apt name." But she noticed that Alex had moved away, turning his head slightly back and forth as he scanned the ground.

"What are you looking for here?" she asked. "Can I help?"

He looked up and gave her a small smile. "You reminded me of something at the post office. When I was a kid, my father used to take me for walks in the woods around the reservation. None of the trees were as old as Junior here." He gestured to the hemlock. "But we used cedar and cottonwood in some of our ceremonies, and when we walked among them, he'd always tell me about how the oldest trees were here before us, and had their own histories outside of ours." He skimmed his hands through his hair. "I should have remembered that. I've forgotten so much."

He went back to scanning, concentrating on the areas where the snow had started to melt. "There, a heel curve." When she came up beside him, he'd crouched down to examine what looked like a partial footprint in the mud, tracing the line with his forefinger where someone's shoe had stamped down into the earth. "A really obvious heel curve." With that, he rose and scanned the ground again. In seconds, he was on the move, and all she could do was follow a few steps behind.

Not too far from Junior, they found a small mound of loose dirt at the base of a much smaller Sitka spruce.

"That looks recent," Alex murmured under his breath as he pulled a hunting knife out of the small pack she hadn't even noticed he'd brought with him. He jammed the blade into the earth, using it and his hands to dig. Before she could even crouch down to help, he'd struck something, the blade clanging against a metal surface. Within seconds, he'd discovered a small metal box, which was unlocked. Inside someone had sealed what looked like a letter in a Ziploc bag.

Alex took it out, and though she was dying to see what it said, she refrained from reading it over his shoulder as he unfolded it. He'd share it with her if he wanted to.

After a few excruciatingly long minutes, he finally finished and stood. "If this is real—" He handed her the paper, which had the Centrix logo— an artful combination of a *C* and an *X* created to resemble northwestern tribal art—at the top. The letter, which was signed by Charles Franklin, the now-deceased Centrix board member that Alex had found in the park, discussed a proposed chemical plant to be built on the Washington peninsula, in the northwest corner near the Strait of Juan de Fuca.

"That's up by Neah Bay," she said. "Near Makah tribal lands."

"Keep reading," Alex said grimly.

The letter went on to describe the proposed site, noting that Centrix had chosen it both for its re-moteness and because it "adhered to criteria for communities least likely to resist the placement of a toxic factory near their homes."

A few paragraphs later, the letter outlined exactly who those communities were:

> …black, rural, Hispanic or Native American communities that demonstrate openness to the promise of economic benefits in exchange for allowing the facilities in the area: residents who are, on average, older than middle age, have a high-school education or less and who are not involved in social issues.

"They're doing it all over again." She shook the letter so the paper rustled in her hand, so incensed by what she'd read that she could hardly speak. "They're targeting the Makah because they think a minority community with its own internal social issues won't put up a fuss about their factory, especially if there are 'economic benefits.'" She didn't even know what to say to that. The greed, the utter lack of respect for human lives and especially for minority communities. It appalled her that people could be so cutthroat over money. Reading between the lines, she wondered if the "waste dump facilities" meant that barrels of poison would start erupting on Makah lands, near Makah schools in a few years.

She got her answer a few sentences later, when she flipped to the next page and found a jargon-filled, emotionless recounting of the dumping that had occurred on Pine Woods lands, noting that as long as proper precautions were taken to prevent "an uprising" like the one that had occurred in South Dakota twenty years earlier, Centrix cleanup and toxic-waste storage costs could be cut considerably. Though the letter writer didn't come out and say the company would start their illegal dumping again, she didn't like the implications behind that sentence at all.

"Your father was behind that 'uprising.' He's what they're trying to prevent." She whirled on him, unable to believe what she'd just read. "Alex, maybe they're the ones coming after you. Rebecca was right—your father was innocent. He has to be."

But she no longer had his attention. He stared at something just over her shoulder and his face had gone completely pale. She took his hand and, her heart hammering loudly in her chest, she turned around slowly, so afraid of what she'd see, of who it was who had followed them.

A few yards away, with the last of the sun's rays behind him and casting his face in shadow, stood a man, his long dark hair pulled back into a ponytail and streaked with gray. He wore a dark brown canvas coat and dark jeans that had probably allowed him to blend in with the trees around him— she certainly hadn't noticed him until he'd stepped into a clear spot.

He took a single step toward them, but she still couldn't make out his features that well in the dimness of the late afternoon. She knew who he was, though, and by his sharp intake of breath behind her, Alex knew, as well.

"Make it public," the man said to them. "And watch your backs." He turned and moved into the trees.

"Wait!" Sophie called. Alex jerked forward and then started to run in the direction in which his father had gone, the expression on his face heartbreaking. But he skidded to a halt a few yards away, and when Sophie caught up to him, she saw that Jack Runningwater had vanished.

"He's gone?" she asked, breathing heavily from her sprint.

Instead of looking at her though, Alex stared intently at the ground. "There." He pointed to a broken stalk that poked through the snow. "Maybe he doesn't know I can track him. No one just vanishes in these woods."

A sharp crack sounded in the air, and reflexively, Alex dove to the ground, hitting her square in the chest and taking her down with him. She caught her tailbone on the root of a tree, falling on her back as Alex landed on top of her. Another shot hit just above their heads, sending a spray of bark raining down on them as Alex rolled her down a small snowy embankment.

He scrambled to his feet, pulling her up beside him. "Run!"

They tore off into the woods, zigzagging through the trees to make it tougher on the shooter. As she batted low-hanging branches and moss out of her face, Sophie tried desperately to keep her footing, stumbling constantly on the unpredictable ground. Stupid shoes. She never should have insisted on coming with him—she was slowing him down, putting him in danger.

Just then, her hand slipped out of his. It only took a few seconds for a distance of several feet to grow between them.

"Sophie!" He slowed down, holding his hand out to her, clearly intending to stop and wait for her.

"Go!" she shouted. "I'm right behind you." Another shot rang out and he ducked down but still wouldn't run. She pushed her legs to go faster, to close the distance between them, but the snow pulled at her legs like cold quicksand. *"Go!"*

She'd just managed to pick up some speed when something stretched out in front of her, catching around her waist and making her feel as if someone had just shot a cannonball into her stomach. She doubled over, struggling to breathe again, and her body jerked to the right as someone yanked her viciously behind one of the larger trees.

And then she was face-to-face with another man—not Alex's father, but a balding, thin man with watery brown eyes and a pleasant half smile on his face. "Well, hello, Miss Brennan."

Her lungs finally opened up and she took a noisy, shuddering breath. She could hear Alex shouting something behind her, but all she cared about at the moment was getting more air.

The man fished inside her coat pocket, extricating the letter she'd carefully tucked away in there. "I'll take that."

He leaned close to her, almost as if he planned to kiss her cheek or hug her goodbye. "Please understand, this isn't personal. But I have to slow your boyfriend down before I kill him."

The pain she'd felt at having the wind knocked out of her was nothing compared to what came next—a jagged, horrible sensation, like having glass pushed through her left side. She clutched her side and dropped to her knees as the man slipped away from her. Stop him. She had to *stop…* She pitched forward, putting out a hand to stop herself from falling face first in the snow. God, it hurt so much. Bright red flowers bloomed on the snow and did a pretty little dance before her eyes. She heard Alex shout her name, felt his arms come across her just as she'd started to fall. Her eyes rolled back and she felt him turning her over, tugging at her jacket and shirt.

"Oh, God, Sophie," his voice said from far, far away.

"It's a trap," she whispered. "It's all a trap." And everything went black.

Chapter Thirteen

When Alex got to her, she was nearly unconscious.

It had taken him barely any time to cross the distance between them, but in those few seconds, she'd been stabbed and left for dead.

Why hadn't he held on to her?

She'd tried to tell him something about a trap, and despite the fact that the gunshots had stopped, he knew they were still in danger. The man who'd attacked her had run into the woods, and Alex didn't know where he'd gone and whether he'd come back.

He heard shouting in the distance, but when he looked around, he couldn't see anything but trees and snow.

"Come on, Sophie." Pulling one of his gloves off with his teeth, he rubbed her cheek, then patted it, trying to get her to come to again. "Please, Sophie."

She stirred and the relief he felt when she opened her eyes was so intense, his own blurred with unshed tears. "Sophie."

"Oh, wow, that hurts."

He gently peeled her hand away from her side and unzipped her jacket. The stab wound beneath looked raw and ugly, blood blooming on her sweater around it. But from what he could tell, it was shallow and close to her side, so it likely hadn't hit any major organs. She'd be fine as long as he could get her to a hospital soon.

He rose, pulling her up with him. "Come on."

"I'll try to walk," she said weakly.

"No, you won't." With that, he reached under her knees and swept her legs from under her, cradling her in his arms. He would have carried her easily, if it hadn't been for the snow catching at his feet with every step. He knew their slow pace made them easy targets and he pushed himself to go faster.

Clinging to him, Sophie gasped every time he stepped too hard and jolted her side. She shook her head. "Alex, I can walk."

But he couldn't put her down. She looked paler than usual, and he knew that despite the stoic front she'd put up, that wound had to hurt like hell. And right now, he would have done anything to ease that, even a little.

Reaching into his pocket, he pulled out his cell phone. "Try calling 911. It might be spotty until we get out from under the tree cover, but keep checking for a signal."

Step by excruciatingly slow step, they finally

made it to the path, where he was able to move faster, though Sophie wasn't able to get reception on his phone. When they stepped out of the trees and into the parking area, Alex couldn't believe what he saw.

The tires on his truck had been slashed, which would make it impossible for them to drive down the mountains themselves. But that wasn't the worst part of it.

On the ground a few yards away from the truck lay a man's body, crumpled in the snow and as still as a pond on a clear day. A sickening rush quickened his pulse and sent a chill across his skin as it hit him that someone had killed his father. But when he moved closer, he saw that the man was a stranger.

"That's the man who stabbed me," Sophie whispered.

This time, there was no stone altar or sheet to mimic the murder of a nun in Ohio, all staged as ritual cult homicides to throw the police off the scent. The man's throat had been cut, his face pale from the loss of blood, his light brown eyes still bulging in surprise. But the upside-down cross inside of a circle had been cut into his chest, just like the two Centrix board members.

Centrix.

Setting Sophie down gently, Alex reached over and tugged at the plastic bag sticking out of the man's jacket pocket. As he'd expected, it contained the letter his father had given him. He took it out of the bag.

Aaron had told him the Ohio murder victim had had an upside-down cross carved on her chest, and that was what they'd seen with the two Centrix murders. But if you came at them from another angle...

It wasn't a cross and circle at all, but an *X* superimposed on top of a *C*—a rudimentary form of the Centrix logo, not easily noticed because of the thick fonts and bright colors Centrix used that made their logo almost a piece of art rather than two letters. But if you distilled it to its simplest form...

Sophie had been right. The murders were related and yet unrelated. Because there were two killers.

Centrix and his father.

He heard the sound of wheels crunching on gravel and turned around, hoping to see the ambulance or a police car driving up to meet them, but knowing that there hadn't been enough time for them to get there.

An expensive-looking black sedan with dark-tinted windows that made it impossible to see inside rolled slowly toward them. When it reached them, the back window facing them rolled down with a faint hum, revealing its passenger—a portly man in his fifties, with a full shock of steel-gray hair and thick, puffy bags under large blue eyes that dominated his face.

"Mr. Gray, I'm Jonathan Wainwright, CEO of Centrix Corporation. I think it's time we had a little talk."

WAINWRIGHT WOULDN'T TELL HIM where they were going—all Alex knew was that they were headed west on 101. He cradled Sophie in his arms and she rested her head on his shoulder, squeezing her side with her eyes closed tightly shut as if in an attempt to block out the pain. Her face still looked pale, and a light sheen of sweat had broken out over her skin, but otherwise she was breathing regularly and her pulse felt strong. He figured they still had some time.

If Wainwright planned to give them time. When he'd noticed the body on the ground back at the park, Wainwright had looked mildly disturbed for a few seconds, saying, "Oh, Robert. How distressing," as if his pet goldfish had just died. The man obviously didn't assign much importance to human lives.

"We need to get her to a doctor," Alex said. He would have preferred to convince the fat man by kicking his teeth in, but Wainwright had brought two men in suits with him, one of whom kept his gun in plain sight. With those two in front of them and Wainwright sitting directly across from them, they weren't in any position to be trying to fight their way out. And that wasn't even counting the driver.

"Mmmmm," Sophie grunted softly as the car went over a bump in the road, jostling all of its passengers. Alex had a small first-aid kit in his pack, and he'd wrapped her side in an elastic bandage and extra gauze. But she'd lost a lot of blood, and he desperately wanted to get her out of there.

"Look, this is between my family and you," he said. "Why don't you tell me what you want? And on the way, we can stop at a hospital and drop off Sophie. She has nothing to do with this."

Wainwright raised a pair of bushy eyebrows at him. "We've been watching you for a long time, Mr. Gray. The minute your father reappeared in Washington, that woman rarely left your side. Of course she had something to do with this. As for how much she knows." The man shrugged. "We don't really care."

Alex sat back hard against the soft leather upholstery. "*We've* been watching, *we* don't care. Who do you think you are, the Queen of England?"

Their portion of the limo was almost like a restaurant booth, with a small table sitting in between two stretches of seats that faced each other. It gave a false intimacy to their conversation, and the close proximity made it easy for Alex to read the big man's expressions. Wainwright wasn't too pleased with him at the moment.

"So what happened to your boy back there?" Alex continued, figuring he might as well try to really tick off the guy before they got to their destination. "He was yours, wasn't he?"

The big man flipped a palm in the air. "Yes. Your father's gained some skill in the past twenty years if he could take down a man like Robert."

"Now here's what I don't get. Why would my

father want to kill Centrix people after all these years? Why didn't he do it sooner?"

Wainwright smacked his tongue against his teeth, considering his response. "I guess it doesn't hurt if you know. Your father somehow managed to infiltrate our corporation a few years ago. He worked as a janitor, of all things." The man laughed, a harsh, gravelly sound. "He had false papers, a fake ID. We never even knew he wasn't who he said he was until he made his move a few months ago. Our security cameras caught him breaking in to my office, where he stole some—how shall we say it?—highly sensitive paperwork."

Alex thought of the letter in his pocket.

"He also cultivated a whistleblower on our board who'd been feeding him information. Now that must've taken years." Wainwright's expression was almost admiring. "When we found out about the stolen documents, he vanished. When we couldn't track him down, we decided to flush him out. And that's when he started going after us."

"Flush him out how?" He knew where this was going, but he wanted to have Wainwright confirm it.

"By going after you and your mother, of course."

Everything his father had done, everything his father had become, had been to get revenge on Centrix. He'd moved to Washington, forged a new identity, gotten a job inside headquarters and had dedicated two decades to getting his revenge.

Without a thought for his family until he'd put them in the worst kind of danger—along with Sophie.

"Years of being a fugitive from the law have really honed his instincts."

It was all starting to fall into place, but there was still one thing Alex didn't get. "What about Wilma Red Cloud?"

Wainwright smiled. "Ask your father."

The car finally rolled to a stop. They'd long ago gotten off the highway and had gone down a well-traveled logging road. Now, they had stopped next to a clear-cut area in the middle of the woods.

The driver got out and came around to Wainwright's side, opening his door for him. As he exited the car, his two sidekicks opened Alex's door. They reached in to pull him out, but he waved them off. "Let me get her," he said, motioning to Sophie.

Putting his arms under her knees and shoulders, he picked her up and carried her from the car, careful to jostle her as little as possible. With the two men flanking him on either side, Alex followed Wainwright through the large clearing, surrounded on all sides by thin cedars that had been planted in careful rows several years ago to create an artificial logging forest.

"I'm very sorry," Wainwright said, not looking sorry at all. "We tried to do this without killing anyone—your mother excepted if she doesn't survive her hospital stay."

If he hadn't been holding Sophie, Alex would have rushed the man.

"But it appears that the only way to tell your father we mean business is for you and your girlfriend here to die." He gestured to one of the men, who pulled out a gun and aimed it at them. Leaning against Alex with her eyes closed, Sophie didn't even seem to notice.

"I don't know if you saw the tan car following us some of the way? Your father should be arriving any minute." Wainwright scanned the tree-lined road from which they'd come. "But you'll be dead, of course. And my men are behind him just waiting for him."

One of the men moved behind him and clamped his hand on Alex's shoulder, pushing him down on his knees. Sophie managed to remain upright, though one look at her told him she might not stay that way for long.

The whole world grew quiet. Wainwright's mouth moved, but Alex couldn't hear anything but the wind rushing through the tree branches, couldn't see anything but the flat, gray brightness of the sky. Colors sharpened and every cell in his body quieted, listening and drinking in everything around him.

He heard Wainwright's man breathing heavily behind him, felt the lightest touch of a gun muzzle against his hairline.

Alex closed his eyes. Sophie.

Snapping his arm into the air, he smacked the

gun away from him and clamped down on the man's wrist. His other hand squeezed the man's fingers, twisting his hand back and away so it bent painfully. With one lightning-quick elbow strike to the groin, Alex incapacitated the man, and in a split second, he was on his feet with the gun pointed directly at Wainwright.

Who had a gun of his own, which he pointed directly at Alex, as did the other man Wainwright had brought with him.

"I suggest you put that down, Mr. Gray," Wainwright said.

"Yeah, I don't think so." He knew the odds were that one of them would end up being hurt worse than Sophie already was. But at least they had a better chance with one of them armed.

He glanced at Sophie, who now sat on the flattened earth. Her eyes were open, which reassured him somewhat. He pulled the gun's hammer back with an audible click. It killed him to see the pained look on her face, so he focused on Wainwright, refusing to believe one or both of them might die in the next few minutes. He'd do everything he could to stop that from happening, to at least give her a fighting chance.

"Put the gun down." She spoke so softly, he barely heard her and chose to ignore it, continuing his standoff with Wainwright and his man.

"Alex, put the gun down."

This time, there was no mistaking her words.

But he couldn't do it. He couldn't just give up their best chance of getting out of there alive, slim as it was. He didn't know why she would think Wainwright wouldn't shoot them the minute the Beretta he held hit the ground.

"Please. Trust me. I told you there'd be a time when I had to help you make a choice. It's now." Holding her side, she pushed up off the ground and rose unsteadily to her feet. She shuffled beside him, putting her hand on his arm. "Put the gun down."

His breath coming out in sharp gasps, Alex couldn't even fathom doing what she'd said. But then again, he'd never heard that kind of strength and sureness in her voice before.

Then she leaned in and whispered, "He's here. He's coming to help you. If you love me, listen to me."

He lowered his arm.

As Wainwright lowered his own gun, ready to leave the task of killing Alex and Sophie to his companion, a voice rang out from the edge of the clearing. "Jonathan Wainwright!"

Alex turned and gave a choked gasp as his father stepped out from the trees. Sophie stumbled against him, clearly having used up her remaining energy, and he wrapped an arm around her to steady her. "Come on, Soph, don't leave me," he whispered, so frightened by the listless, faraway look in her eyes.

"Well, Jack." Wainwright spoke as if greeting an old friend. "Here I thought you'd disappeared, and all this time, we've been friends and I didn't know it."

"Your cleaning people aren't your friends. You don't even see them." Runningwater walked up the slight rise toward them, and Alex saw his father's face clearly for the first time in two decades. "Let them go. I'll stay behind."

Wainwright tilted his head to the side, pressing a finger against his jowly cheek as if pretending to give Runningwater's statement some thought. "No, I don't think so. You've been a thorn in our side for such a long time. I wouldn't want to take the chance that your son inherited those tendencies."

"I knew you'd be that greedy," Runningwater said. With that, he raised his arm and a group of dark-skinned men stepped out of the trees from which he'd come. Then another group came out behind them. They fanned out, raising their rifles, the air a cacophony of clacking sounds as they ratcheted shells into the rifle chambers.

"Let me introduce you to my friends, the members of the Makah tribal police," Jack said, his mouth twisted up in a satisfied smile. "They've been wanting to meet you for a long time."

Chapter Fourteen

When Wainwright had finally realized he'd lost, Jack Runningwater had walked back into the woods and let the Makah police take care of the CEO. Alex wondered what would happen to his father now that the thing that had driven him for two decades was gone. In a highly publicized event, Jonathan Wainwright had been turned over to the Seattle FBI office, which was now investigating him and several members of the Centrix board of directors for multiple counts of fraud, conspiracy and, of course, attempted murder. The evening news said the whole thing could be the end of the corporation altogether, much like what had happened to Enron.

None of it, however, served to clear his father's name of the murder of Wilma Red Cloud. And since the man had disappeared without a backward glance at his son, Alex had no way of contacting him to see what the story really had been.

But it didn't matter anymore. His mother had finally recovered, and after a long week of waiting for the anesthesia to completely leave her system, she'd finally come home.

Alex unlocked her house, placed her small travel bag inside the front door and held it open so she could come inside.

"Ah, it's good to be home," she said, looking around her familiar kitchen with a satisfied smile. "And you cleaned up the kitchen. I was worried about all those baking pans left to fester."

"Oh, they festered," he said. "But I handled it." He closed the door and they went into the small living room just beyond the kitchen. "You know, I could stay here tonight, if you need some company—"

"Ohhh." She waved a dismissive hand at him as she sat down on her sage-green sofa. He sat beside her. "No, you go home. I'm fine."

"But I thought you might—"

"Be upset about your father?" She reached out, brushing a hand tenderly against his cheek. "No. I worked through all of that a long time ago." Sitting back against the plush cushions, she finger-combed her hair, a faraway look in her eyes.

"Did you ever see him, after we left the reservation?" he asked. Talking about it didn't seem to bother her, but maybe she'd shoved her feelings down deep, the way Alex had. And after all she'd been through, she was the last person he wanted to upset.

"We left to follow him. He went where Centrix

had its headquarters," she said. "He contacted me a few times early on, but I eventually figured out he wasn't just hiding from the police. His revenge against Centrix consumed him—it became more important than his family." She glanced at him. "He just stopped being the man I loved, so I let him go."

If only it were that easy. It would have been, if he hadn't seen the man, if he'd been able to keep hiding from the memories he'd had of the six years during which he'd had a father. But it all felt raw and immediate, as if he'd been abandoned by one parent all over again.

"Let him go, Alex."

Easier said than done.

Just then, he heard a knock at the door.

"Is that Sophie? I told her to come over today," Anna said. "I'm so glad you've finally found a nice girl instead of the bimbos you used to bring home."

Sophie had spent a couple of days in the hospital herself, recovering from her stab wound. He'd introduced her to his mother and the two of them had hit it off immediately. Between his mother, her recovery, work and his own need to be alone and process what had happened, he hadn't seen much of Sophie in the past few days. And knowing she stood right outside his mother's door brought home how much he'd missed her.

He pulled open the door.

"Hi." She gave him that little wave of hers. "Thought I'd come see how Anna was doing."

Gripping the lapels of her jacket, he pulled her to him and kissed her, loving the surprised squeak she made before her arms went around him and she pressed that soft, incredible body up against his. When they finally broke apart, both of them were breathing heavily. He noticed his mother, who had been close behind him when he'd gone to answer the door, had suddenly disappeared.

"So, miss me a little?" She laughed.

He grinned at her. "A lot."

"I didn't miss you at all." Her mouth quivered with barely suppressed laughter. "I mean, I have my books, classes, the Neighborhood Watch. And I think Mr. Finkelstein two doors down has a thing for me."

He raised an eyebrow. "Oh, really?"

"Yes. It's getting serious."

He shut the door behind him and pulled her back into his arms. "Tell him I'm putting up a fight. My mom is already asking when I'm going to make you her daughter-in-law."

Her eyes widened in surprise. "Hmmm?"

He bent his head, dropping a soft kiss on her neck. "I told her I had to take you on a real date first."

"A date. That might be nice."

"But then I said that I'm so crazy in love with you, that maybe on our second date I'd let you talk me into it."

She pressed her palms against his chest, pushing back to look at him. "Alex?"

"I love you," he said softly. "Thank you for everything you did for me."

"I didn't do much—"

"No, you just got yourself arrested, skipped a bunch of classes, probably wrote the world's most incoherent term paper at the hotel—" She blushed, obviously thinking of what they'd done at the hotel. "You got stabbed, nearly died. And all because you wanted to help me." He leaned forward, touching his forehead to hers. "Thank you."

She glanced down for a few seconds, silent, and when she finally looked back up at him, he noticed that her eyes were glistening. "You'll need to go back to that tree. I don't know when, but I think you'll know."

"Well, that was random." And not the response he'd been hoping for.

"Are you sure you can put up with that?" She rolled her eyes. "I'm *always* random."

He bit his lower lip and grinned at her. "I'm not going anywhere."

She threw her arms around his neck. "I love you, too," she whispered.

Epilogue

On the day that Centrix CEO Jonathan Wainwright was indicted for two counts of attempted murder and conspiracy to commit murder, Alex went on a hike by himself in Renegade Ridge State Park. Maybe Sophie was rubbing off on him, but as soon as he stepped around a turn in the path and saw the western hemlock they called Junior up ahead, he knew he wasn't alone.

Stepping up to the ancient tree's roots, he braced himself with one hand against its rough bark and waited under its moss-draped branches. Amid the normal noises of the rainforest—the soft calls of a hundred different birds, the sound of the wind rushing through pine boughs and rustling decaying leaves, the scratch of a squirrel skittering along a branch—he heard the softest of aberrations, the snap of the slightest twig.

When he turned, a man stood where none had been before, his long black hair blown away from his face by a gentle breeze. There was no mistaking that face—it was his own in a few decades' time.

"Alex," the man said, as if his name were a sacred thing. He would have replied, but he had no words for that moment, one he'd waited and not waited for all his life.

They remained like that for a long time, and Alex found himself wishing he could just freeze time and be there with his father, instead of asking the question he had to ask. "Did you kill those men?" His voice sounded faraway and hoarse, as if it belonged to someone else.

"There are some things you shouldn't know, son," Runningwater replied. And Alex suddenly found himself wishing they could get back all the years that stretched between them like a chasm, wasted on one man's misguided quest for vengeance. Some would consider the man a hero—he had no doubt Rebecca Red Cloud would be one of them. But the law considered him a murderer, no better than the Centrix board members who had consigned hundreds of Lakota to death.

Alex swallowed, trying to get rid of the lump that had lodged in his throat. "No matter what your motives were, you shouldn't have taken the law into your own hands. You're a murderer, just like they are."

His father's face darkened. "I did what I had to do."

Alex pressed his palm harder against the tree trunk, letting Methuselah Jr. hold him up. "You should have gone to the police."

Shaking his head, Runningwater laughed, a loud, bitter sound that hinted at what his life had become in the last twenty years. "You think the government would have helped? We tried twenty years ago to get them to hear us, and they turned away," he said. "They killed Lakota at Wounded Knee for a ghost dance a century ago, and they did the same thing when they let Centrix poison our land and refused to do anything about it. It was a quieter form of genocide, but the intent was the same."

"You killed those men."

"I protect my own." He pointed at Alex. "And you're my own. You're a Runningwater, even if you call yourself Gray."

Alex closed his eyes, wishing he'd never come here to have this conversation. Wishing his father had remained the evil caricature he'd grown up believing him to be, and not this flesh and blood man with love as his motivation for the blood on his hands. Something Wainwright had said to him had been haunting him since that day in Neah Bay. Though he didn't want to ask, he knew he had to. "What happened to Wilma Red Cloud?"

Bowing his head, Jack sighed deeply. "Centrix paid her off."

When Alex opened his eyes again, Jack stood

directly in front of him, close enough to touch. "She knew about the dumping?"

"She made it possible," he said. "And was paid well to do so."

If Wilma had been in league with the corporation all along, it didn't seem likely that they would have killed her. Which only left one option. "Who killed her, Jack?" The name sounded off when he said it, but Alex calling the man *Dad* just didn't seem like an option.

Squeezing the bridge of his nose, his father worked his jaw. "I did," he said finally.

He'd been expecting that, somehow, but it didn't make it any easier to hear.

"I was a member of the tribal police, and during another investigation, I heard something I wasn't supposed to hear." He frowned, lost in the past. "I confronted her, she pulled out a gun, and I had to defend myself."

"You strangled her?" He felt sick and all he wanted to do was get away from this man, to pretend that someone like him couldn't be related to him.

Jack's head snapped up, his dark eyes flashing in anger. "She had a gun, Alex, which she was ready to use. And her greed had killed so many on Pine Woods. Children. It wasn't difficult to conjure up enough rage to commit that act." He looked away. "Don't worry—I didn't enjoy what I did. Part of the reason I left you and your mother was because I couldn't face you anymore, after what I'd done."

And just like that, Alex found himself almost believing the man, almost justifying his actions in his mind. He knew it was the lonely six-year-old rearing up inside him again, but it didn't make the emotional train wreck any easier to bear. "If it was self-defense, you should have turned yourself in. Maybe—"

"Maybe I'd still be in jail." He gave Alex a wry smile, with absolutely no mirth behind it. "With a multibillion-dollar company wanting to put me away? I'd been a thorn in their side for a long time. I have no doubt they could have bought a judge."

The letters. The torched lab. And the publicity, which was starting to become nationwide by the time his father had committed murder. No doubt Centrix management would have wanted Jack Runningwater to go away. And they'd already demonstrated that Lakota lives meant very little to them.

"But now? You might have a chance now." He heard and hated the desperation in his voice.

Jack shook his head. "Alex, I'm not going anywhere. I killed Wilma Red Cloud. I killed those board members. Nothing is going to make that all right." Then he straightened, standing tall, and Alex could see exactly how a man like him could be dangerous. "And I'm not serving a day in jail for Centrix."

"I should turn you in." He believed in the U.S. justice system, but he could understand why his father wouldn't. That understanding, however, didn't make him any more eager to be an accomplice to Jack Runningwater's second great escape. "You committed murder."

"If that's what you feel is right," Jack replied simply.

Alex stepped toward him, not quite knowing what he was going to do. But once he got close enough, emotion took over, and he just embraced his father. "Dad," he said, his voice breaking. Jack hugged him back fiercely.

"I'm sorry, Alex. I'm so sorry," he murmured over and over.

God, after everything that had happened, all Alex wanted to do was play basketball again with his father.

They'd never have a casual conversation. For all he knew, this could be the last time Jack would be this close. Five minutes from now, ten, he could go back to being the invisible man in Alex's life. Always invisible.

He held on until he couldn't anymore, and then straightened, blinking back unfamiliar tears that threatened to blind him. "How did you manage to elude the cops all these years?"

He saw the deep sadness he felt reflected in the older man. "Desperate men have desperate ways," he replied. "You don't need to know more than that."

He became hyperaware of the glare of the setting sun on the snow, the feel of the crisp, cold breeze on his face, the sound of the tree branches rustling overhead, every sound and every sensation preserving itself forever in his memory. "It's as if someone looks away from you for a minute, you just disappear." And then he slowly and deliberately turned his back on Jack.

When he finally turned back around, Jack was gone, the only trace of him a set of tracks in the snow that Alex wouldn't follow.

He leaned his head against Junior's rough bark, his vision blurring until all he could see was a haze of brown and black. He didn't know how long he'd stood like that, but suddenly he felt a pair of soft arms encircle his waist. He sighed, relaxing into Sophie's strong embrace.

"I'm sorry," she said into his back.

He remained like that for a while, lost in his thoughts and drinking in the comfort she offered. Finally, he turned in her arms to face her. "I'm fine."

She wagged her eyebrows at him. "Yes, you are fine."

He couldn't help but laugh at her. "Ah, that's my girl."

Her expression grew serious. "Do you think you'll see him again?"

He shrugged. "What's the point?"

She brushed her fingers along his hairline. "The point is, he's your father. No matter what. Even though his priorities are really screwed up."

"I don't know."

She stood on her toes, brushing a kiss on his cheek. "Well, you have your mother. And I'm here."

Her words soothed the raw, exposed place his father had left, and he knew that whether he saw Jack again or not, whether law enforcement caught up with him or not, he'd be just fine. "Then that's all I need."

* * * * *

Kimberley Blackstone didn't notice the waiting horde of media until it was too late. Flashbulbs exploded around her like a New Year's light show. She skidded to a halt, so abruptly her trailing suitcase all but overtook her.

This had to be a case of mistaken identity. Surely. Kimberley hadn't been on the paparazzi hit list for close to a decade, not since she'd estranged herself from her billionaire father and his headline-hungry diamond business.

But no, it was *her* name they called. *Her* face was the focus of a swarm of lenses that circled her like avid hornets. Her heart started to pound with fear-fueled adrenaline.

What did they want?

What was going on?

With a rising sense of bewilderment she scanned the crowd for a clue, and her gaze fastened on a tall, leonine figure forcing his way to the front. A tall, familiar figure. Her head came up in stunned recognition, and their gazes collided across the sea of heads before the cameras erupted with another barrage of flashes, this time right in her exposed face.

Blinded by the flashbulbs—and by the shock of that momentary eye-meet—Kimberley didn't realize his intent until he'd forged his way to her side, possibly by the sheer strength of his personality. She felt his arm wrap around her shoulder, pulling her into the protective shelter of his body, allowing her no time to object. No chance to lift her hands to ward him off.

In the space of a hastily drawn breath, she found herself plastered knee-to-nose against six feet two inches of hard-bodied male.

Ric Perrini.

Her lover for ten torrid weeks, her husband for ten tumultuous days.

Her ex for ten tranquil years.

After all this time, he should not have felt so familiar but, oh dear, he did. She knew the scent of that body and its lean, muscular strength. She knew its heat and its slick power and every response it could draw from hers.

She also recognized the ease with which he'd

taken control of the moment and the decisiveness of his deep voice when it rumbled close to her ear. "I have a car waiting outside. Is this your only luggage?"

Kimberley nodded. "I assume you will tell me," she said tightly, "what this welcome party is all about."

"Not while the welcome party is within earshot. No."

Barking a request for the cameramen to stand aside, Perrini took her hand and pulled her into step with his ground-eating stride. Kimberley let him, because he was right, damn his arrogant, Italian-suited hide. Despite the speed with which he whisked her across the airport terminal, she could almost feel the hot breath of the pursuing media on her back.

This was neither the time nor the place for explanations. Inside his car, however, she would get answers.

Now that the initial shock had been blown away—by the haste of their retreat, by the heat of her gathering indignation, by the rush of adrenaline fired by Perrini's presence and the looming verbal battle—her brain was starting to tick over. This had to be her father's doing. And if it was a Howard Blackstone publicity ploy, then it had to be about Blackstone Diamonds, the company that ruled his life.

The knowledge made her chest tighten with a familiar ache of disillusionment.

She'd known her father would be flying in from Sydney for today's opening of the newest in his chain of exclusive, high-end jewelry boutiques. The opulent shop front sat adjacent to the rival business where Kimberley worked. No coincidence, she thought bitterly, just as it was no coincidence that Ric Perrini was here in Auckland ushering her to his car.

Perrini was Howard Blackstone's right-hand man, second in command at Blackstone Diamonds, a legacy of his short-lived marriage to the boss's daughter. No doubt her father had sent him to fetch her; the question was *why?*

* * * * *

Get swept away down under with the glitz and glamour of the Blackstone empire as Kimberley tries to determine the real reason behind her "reunion" with Ric....

Look for VOWS & A VENGEFUL GROOM
by Bronwyn Jameson
in stores January 2008.

When Kimberley Blackstone's father is presumed dead, Kimberley is required to take over the helm of Blackstone Diamonds. She has to work closely with her ex, Ric Perrini, to battle not only the press, but also the fierce attraction still sizzling between them. Does Ric feel the same...or is it the power her share of Blackstone Diamonds will provide him as he battles for boardroom supremacy.

Look for

VOWS & A VENGEFUL GROOM

by

BRONWYN JAMESON

Available January wherever you buy books

nocturne™

Jachin Black always knew he was an outcast.
Not only was he a vampire, he was a vampire
banished from the Sanguinas society. Jachin, forced
to survive among mortals, is determined to buy
his way back into the clan one day.

Ariel Swanson, debut author of a vampire novel, could
be the ticket he needs to get revenge and take his
rightful place among the Sanguinas again. However,
the unsuspecting mortal woman has no idea of the
dark and sensual path she will be forced to travel.

Look for

RESURRECTION: THE BEGINNING

by

PATRICE MICHELLE

Available January 2008 wherever you buy books.

Visit Silhouette Books at www.eHarlequin.com   SN61778

ATHENA FORCE

Heart-pounding romance and thrilling adventure.

CAUGHT IN THE CROSS FIRE

Francesca Thorn is the FBI's best profiler...and she's needed to target Athena Academy's most dangerous foe. But as she gets dangerously close to revealing the identity of her alma mater's greatest threat, someone will stop at nothing to ensure she remains dead silent. Her only choice is to accept all the help her irritatingly sexy U.S. Army bodyguard can provide.

ATHENA FORCE

Will the women of Athena unravel Arachne's powerful web of blackmail and death…or succumb to their enemies' deadly secrets?

Look for

MOVING TARGET

by *Lori A. May,*

H107

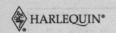

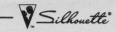

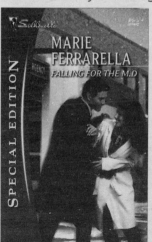

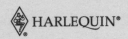

INTRIGUE

COMING NEXT MONTH

6 heroes. 6 stories. One month to read them all.

www.eHarlequin.com

HICNM1207